_____ A FALLING STAR _____

Marseahna came to a sudden halt as she entered the clearing where she had expected to see the remains of a falling star. Her mouth dropped open as she stared at the strangely shaped metal object being sucked into the black water of the marsh, the steam rising from it in vapors and hissing like some writhing snake. Marseahna risked moving a step closer, only to stand in shaking, paralyzed fear as part of the blackened metal began to move upward, leaving a gaping hole in the top.

As she watched mutely, a human form emerged, unsteadily and yet with purpose, for it disappeared again and then reappeared, holding another form close to it. The capsule bobbed jerkily to one side, dipping down low toward the slimy murk that was pulling it under. Suddenly Marseahna was running toward the object that was beginning to disappear beneath the surface of the marsh . . .

THE PATH OF EXOTERRA

GORDON McBAIN

AVON
PUBLISHERS OF BARD, CAMELOT AND DISCUS BOOKS

THE PATH OF EXOTERRA is an original publication of Avon Books. This work has never before appeared in book form.

AVON BOOKS
A division of
The Hearst Corporation
959 Eighth Avenue
New York, New York 10019

First Avon Printing, May, 1981

AVON TRADEMARK REG. U.S. PAT. OFF. AND IN OTHER COUNTRIES, MARCA REGISTRADA, HECHO EN U.S.A.

Printed in the U.S.A.

Dedicated to my sister, Laurie McBain.
With love, always.

Prince Orion traced the constellations that crowned the night sky. For a brief moment his green eyes lingered on a dim star, and a strange apprehension enveloped him. For on a small planet orbiting that star, his destiny would be changed forever when he crossed the path of Exoterra.

CHAPTER 1

The vision of the planet Verdana and its three moons filled Truestar with relief as he slowed his starship, the *Eagalos,* to sublight speed and the universe came into focus once again. Here on this planet, an outpost of primitive humans, he planned to find a safe haven far from the turmoil that had led to his sudden flight from home.

After flashing like a meteor through the Verdana night skies, Truestar piloted the *Eagalos* to the planet's surface, hovering in midair dangerously close to the murky waters of a swamp pool. Quickly the scientist activated his ship's tractor beam. Soon a mysterious rock was lowered from the cargo hold into the depths of the boggy waters. As the last portion of the rock sank in the swampy mire, Truestar wiped his sweaty brow and uttered a sigh of relief that echoed through the cabin of his ship.

Suddenly Truestar was jolted by the beeping of his ship's scanner. The instrument was showing that twelve small fragments had broken from the main stone during its descent. They now lay exposed on the floor of the fern forest that surrounded the swamp pool! Knowing that even a fragment of the unique stone could be dangerous in the wrong hands, Truestar realized instantly that he would have to recover the stones. But dawn was near and he could not risk being seen. His only alternative was to pilot the *Eagalos* to the nearby mountain range and descend into the maze of caverns that few knew existed. Not even the inhabitants of the closest Verdanan village, Theos, knew of the strange human-carved caverns that had been left by an earlier expedition.

It had been the knowledge of these caverns that convinced Truestar to choose Verdana as his destination when he was forced to take his sudden solo flight. With finesse Truestar lowered his ship into the mountain caverns just as Verdana's star rose over the mountain rims. As he unloaded his supplies in the eerie lighting left by the long-lost colonists from another time, Truestar formulated his plans to leave at nightfall on foot to recover the lost twelve fragments.

Only Desera, third moon of Verdana, was still visible in the dawning heavens, its faint light shadowing the hawklike features of a lone figure trudging purposefully toward the inhospitably steep ridge of rock that towered above the valley floor. The sun was traveling high in the cloudless sky when Truestar finally allowed himself a moment's respite from his forced march from the fern forest far below.

He hesitated for a second, then pulled a slim metal box from a fold in the pocket beneath his cloak. Studying the box with his keen gray eyes, Truestar emptied the contents into his other hand and fingered the small stone fragments that gleamed with turquoise splendor in the rays of high noon.

"Eleven," he muttered beneath his breath as he counted them in growing dismay. "I could have sworn that the ship's sensors registered an even dozen." He considered returning to search for the missing crystal, which might be there in the marshlands below.

But he knew he could not go back. Truestar chided himself for his carelessness in allowing that villager to come upon him so unexpectedly this morning. He had mistakenly assumed himself to be safe, deep within the bog-infested boundaries of the swamps. But as he was recovering the small fragments of stone that morning, he had been startled by the sudden appearance of a village girl who had strayed deep into the swamps.

Who had been more astounded by the unexpected meeting, he did not know, although he would guess it had been the Verdanan girl. She had cried out and taken to her heels upon seeing the cloaked figure crouching before her, disappearing into a clump of tall marsh reeds. Before the long grasses had stopped their wild undulating and the villager had found the courage to peer out, Truestar had vanished.

Now the sun was disappearing into the sea as Truestar came upon the fork in the path where the entrance to his cavern sanctuary was disguised. With a sigh of tired satisfaction Truestar threw back his hood, the last dying rays of the sun catching the strong features of his face, which was framed by thick gray hair. He wiped the sweat from his lined brow; then, glancing around almost furtively, he pressed a button by the buckle of his belt and a large boulder at the base of the escarpment slid back, closing again after allowing him only seconds to pass into the mouth of the dark cave beyond. With the sudden disappearance of the long-robed figure, the mountain seemed undisturbed as before.

In the glow of the flare lamps in the main cavern the Exoterra crystals shone eerily. How could something so beautiful be so powerful? Truestar pondered as he stared down at them in his open palm. He clutched the stones tightly in his hands as he thought of his sudden flight from his native sector of space. He recalled how he and the other scientists on the survey outpost, Geometral, had captured a rogue planetoid, and during intensive testing learned that the crystals, when activated, could yield seemingly infinite power. And though the meteor could be fragmented, the crystals themselves could not be destroyed.

From that point on, the meteor became known as the Exoterra Stone, for the word Exoterra meant a strange power from beyond the edge of the Known Worlds.

The excitement of the discovery of the stone and its fantastic powers spread rapidly throughout the planets of Confederation space. But news leaked as well to L'Juntara, the dictator of a rival planetary alliance.

11

Worried that the new power would revolutionize Confederation strength, L'Juntara launched a surprise attack against Geometral. In the midst of the attack, a lone starship had escaped into deep space, carrying its single passenger, Truestar, the chief Confederation scientist, and his cargo—the Exoterra Stone.

After concealing the stones in the metal box, Truestar stretched out wearily on the small cot he had set up next to his starship. Before falling asleep Truestar activated the portable visiscreen, training the cameras hidden beyond the cavern entrance into the Verdana sky. The twin moons, Ahna and Seahna, were in full view, and Desera was a sliver just beginning to rise above the Tor Cloudtopt range.

Truestar gazed beyond the moons to the millions of stars and located the familiar sector of Confederation space. A sudden sadness filled him as he thought of his people, especially Stellara, the woman he was soon to have married. But all that must wait for now, Truestar thought as he turned off the screen and drifted into a troubled sleep. He had only one purpose now, and that was to keep the Exoterra Stone away from L'Juntara and to discover the means to destroy this stone that now lay buried in the swamp.

How tragic it would be to have to destroy the stone, Truestar thought, knowing how its unique powers could have been used in a positive manner to strengthen the Confederate alliance or to improve the lives of millions of people by warming planets undergoing negative climatic changes.

But the scientist in Truestar gave way to the committed rebel fighting for the life of his Confederation. He knew that if the Exoterra Stone fell into L'Juntara's hands, the Confederation would face ultimate annihilation by so awesome a power. Thus far survival for the Confederate worlds had been won with grave losses and brave sacrifice by the citizens. It was a constant struggle to survive, and to possess the Exoterra Stone could very

12

well decide the fate of countless billions in the galaxy who had joined together in a common cause of freedom. And whether their struggle continued to succeed now rested with a solitary stone, now buried in a murky bog on a primitive world.

CHAPTER 2

The sun had risen high above Marseahna's head before she finally peeked from her hiding place and took a quick look around her. She was still alive. Marseahna expelled a shuddering sigh of thankfulness and very, very quietly struggled to her knees, her muscles stiff from her prolonged inactivity. She crawled forward and cautiously peered between the fronds of the tall grasses, but there was only a silent, empty clearing to be surveyed. Marseahna now bravely stepped from her concealment and stared around the deserted clearing in growing amazement. She rubbed her raven-black eyes with the back of her hands, unsure for a moment if she had really seen that strange hooded figure.

Suddenly a bright gleam of turquoise nearly blinded Marseahna. At first she just stared, immobilized by the strange glow, then slowly she bent down to examine more closely the source of such a brilliant, beautiful color. Her shaking fingers scraped through the mud and touched the small turquoise crystal. She started in surprise at its peculiar coldness; then, picking it up, she rubbed it clean on her woolen tunic. Her eyes darted in every direction, lest the hooded figure return to claim his valuable property—now in her possession.

Marseahna sat in the quiet of the swamp for quite a while as she turned the stone over and over in her palm, putting it up to her dark eyes to gaze almost hypnotically into its vivid blue-green depths. Even the Aquagran, the endless sea that bordered Theos, her village, on the west, seemed dull compared to the prize she had found.

"The festival!" Marseahna cried, her excited voice startling the swamp creatures. She jumped to her feet, sending a flock of wild birds into the blue sky, but Marseahna was too preoccupied to notice. "The festival." She spoke again. "This will be my gift to the high priests of the god. Tomorrow night when they once again land their fiery ship on the sands of the Aquagran, I, Marseahna, will have the most beautiful gift to offer." But then, in a more cautious moment, she decided not to tell them about the figure she had seen. They might think it wrong to have seen him, and to have strayed so far from the village. "Nothing must tarnish the value of my gift," Marseahna said to herself with a pleased smile.

She secured the small treasure in her tunic pocket and then swiftly made her way back from the marshes, frequently casting nervous glances over her shoulder whenever she thought she heard a furtive movement in the underbrush. The breeze tossed her waist-length raven hair as she reached the security of her small thatched cottage in the rolling farmlands that bordered the swamp.

Since her parents had died in the plague that had ravaged Verdana's population two years earlier, Marseahna had lived alone on the border of the swamp. Tired from her endless days spent tending her crop of Burganberries, that fruit so relished by Verdanans, she had had little time or energy for the nighttime social gatherings in Theos. This shunning of the almost compulsory attendance at events, and especially her disinterest in the amorous advances by the most eligible of the village's young men, had caused Marseahna to be viewed with a certain degree of suspicion. The superstitious villagers could not comprehend why one so young and beautiful would choose to live alone in the swamp shadows outside the heavy wooden gates of Theos that protected those who lived within from attacks by tribes of nomadic bandits.

But Marseahna was different. She knew only gentle ways, both with swamp creatures and bandits. She might not be content with her lot in life, but she did manage a comfortable living peddling her Burganberries in the village square, from which they ultimately found their way into the much-beloved Burganberry nectar. She had always felt that her gift of Burganberry nectar had more than pleased the priests. In fact, the priests seemed to have an unquenchable thirst for the Verdanan drink. Other villagers often bartered the goods they made with her so that they could also present nectar to the priests.

Marseahna was nevertheless subject to the hostility and mistrust of the villagers, and she naively viewed the turquoise crystal as the means of fostering warmer relations with them. For who could possibly shun one who gave such a beautiful gift to the priests of the god?

Marseahna glanced up into the starlit sky, watching in fascination as Desera rose higher over Tor Cloudtopt while the twin moons, for which she was named, filled her farm with bluish light. Her dark eyes reflected the wide, endless sky as she stared up at the millions of pinpoints of light twinkling above her head.

CHAPTER 3

The golden sands of the Aquagran had long ago faded in the deepening dusk of twilight. The waters had turned from turquoise to indigo as darkness had fallen. The villagers feasted, their laughter carried away with the wind, and most were now settled down on mats and coarse blankets along the shoreline as they awaited the arrival of the priests.

It was with some fear that the villagers awaited these visitors and their fiery vehicle. The ancient chronicles of Theos were filled with images of battles among the stars and cities set to flame by light beams from chariots in the sky. It was this foreboding that led the villagers of Verdana to greet the space travelers on their first visit as dieties to be appeased, not angered. Since the visit had proved no cause for alarm, in subsequent visits the Verdanans continued their policy of greeting the priest ship with offerings, hoping never to anger the god and have their villages destroyed in clouds of flame, as in the old chronicles.

Marseahna saw the star before the village elder did. But it was customary for the council chief to rise to his feet and point heavenward, announcing the arrival of the priests. It was the way it had always happened, and was the signal for the other villagers to rise and stare at the pinpoint of light which seemed at first to be just another bright star in the heavens, until it started to move and grow in size before gliding downward from the skies of Verdana. Even though they had seen this ship many times before, a gasp and murmur spread through the crowd of villagers as the light took symmetrical shape and a distant roar drowned out the sound of the sea waves splashing against the shore.

19

The villagers waited nervously in an unnatural silence until finally there was a whooshing of air, and a portal in the side of the ship opened to reveal two white-robed figures, their faces effectively concealed by hoods. In the strange shadowy glow of the spacecraft, the seven-foot-tall figures of the priests were imbued with an other-worldly enchantment that kept the primitive villagers spellbound.

One of the priests gestured with his outstretched arm and the assembled villagers fell to their knees in the sand in their accustomed response, while the other priest moved along the row of offerings from the villagers of Theos. Imperiously he beckoned to several of the nearby villagers and they hurried forward to load the gifts on to the bottom of the ramp that had slid down from the opened portal of the ship.

The first priest put a small box to his lips, and soon his deep bass voice boomed over the crowd. "Citizens of Theos, once again the priests of the god L'Juntara thank you for these offerings. We convey his blessing to you, his most loyal people. He will continue to protect your village from harm. Now we will leave you, and . . ." but his voice trailed off as one of the villagers suddenly jumped to her feet and bravely approached the robed figures. The priest raised a loose-sleeved arm commandingly, his gesture halting the villager in her tracks. "You dare to rise and face the priest of L'Juntara without permission?" he demanded in a harsh but curious voice staring down at the cowering young woman.

The priests were not the only ones to notice the brilliant sparkle of the turquoise stone glowing in the palm of Marseahna's outstretched hand. Many of the villagers were now craning their necks to see what it was that Marseahna had dared to offer to the god from her own hand. With a swishing of his robe the priest who had been overseeing the loading of the other gifts now rushed over to stand beside his colleague as he stared down at the blue-green stone that burned with inner fire. Their hooded heads were suddenly bent close together as they conferred; then the one who had spoken raised his arms heavenward.

Marseahna had fallen back onto her knees before the priest, her heart stilled in her breast as she trembled under the eyes she could feel staring down at her from the darkness of those hooded figures. A paralyzing chill spread through her body at the thought that she had somehow displeased the priest. She wished with every breath that she was back in the safety of her Burganberry farm, free from their penetrating scrutiny.

"The god thanks you for your gift most of all, young villager," spoke the deep voice, cutting through the tense silence. "Come forward and present it to me."

Marseahna was ushered forward and then into the portal of the starship. The villagers stared in growing disbelief as the portal closed. They waited in stunned silence for one of their kind to emerge from the sacred ship.

After what seemed an endless vigil, the portal reopened and a dazed Marseahna walked out and fell onto the sand, her eyes gazing blankly upward into the heavens.

One of the priests followed her out of the portal and addressed the villagers. "See that no harm comes to her. She has been awed by the sight of the god. She has not been harmed. Return her to her farm at once."

With that command the priest reentered the starship, and soon the sound of the engines rose over the Aquagran. Sands began to swirl around the still-stunned villagers, who shielded their eyes as the ship ascended and was soon lost in the myriad of star clusters in the Verdana sky.

CHAPTER 4

The monstrous star cruiser had left its orbit of the planet Verdana and sped hyperlight toward Space Station ACXII located on the fringes of the official Juntarium space. The cruiser personnel had waited anxiously while the priests in the shuttle had docked before breaking orbit and jumping into hyperspace for the journey to the space station.

Now the forms on the bridge visiscreen lost their mystical shapes and began to solidify as the ship slowed to sublight speed again and the universe came into familiar focus. Off to the left of the screen, a large shimmering figure began to grow more distinct as it dominated the screen before mushrooming into its man-made shape. It looked like a giant spoked wheel floating in open space. The cruiser drew nearer, and soon it was dwarfed by the awesome space station.

The cruiser docked inside the opened portal of one of the many hangar decks stacked within the shelter of one of the spokes. The roar of the engines filled the cavernous hangar; then there was silence as the cruiser came to rest, the portal closing silently against the blackness of space. The two priests descended the ramp and were instantly engulfed by a busy horde of minor officials. One of the priests was carrying a tiny metal box held very closely—indeed, almost possessively—beneath his arm as he disappeared into the depths of the station.

Soon the crew of the recently docked cruiser joined the rest of the station personnel in the crowd that was forming on the hangar deck for an unexpected announcement. But the wave of excitement breaking through the crowd was not for the docking of a cruiser.

It had been some time since most had seen the powerful, charismatic leader of the Juntarium forces, L'Juntara. Their memories flashed on the vision of the tall bearded figure who had first unified the savagely fighting factions of his home world, Juntar, then conquered other, more primitive planets, and now had expanded his empire to adjacent star systems. These conquered worlds were for the most part poor, underdeveloped human colonies that had few defenses against a more advanced adversary. Their resistance was dealt with severely, and now they were under ruthless Juntarium subjugation.

The crowd grew suddenly silent as the station stargate once again opened to admit a docking starship. This ship was much the same as the other, with its sleek metallic exterior, except for the symbol of L'Juntara, a scarlet planet encircled by tiny dots, which were connected to the mother planet by flames shooting out from its surface.

L'Juntara's ship came to rest, the steady throb of its engines fading into the cavernous silence of the hangar. Then the ship's portal opened, and an entire battalion of guards quickly emerged to station themselves around the ship's ramp in an orderly row. They stood at attention, the best troopers of L'Juntara, their sole purpose to protect their leader, by risking their own lives if necessary. Dressed in full battle gear, their silvery-black lightweight metal vests partially concealed beneath long capes thrown back over their shoulders, they instilled fear even among their own armies. Taller than average, they stood staring straight ahead, with gloved hands on their weapons, prepared to counter any sudden attack or assassination attempt upon their leader. Mutely they waited, their faces masked behind steel nose guards, their heads covered by protective helmets bearing the insignia of L'Juntara.

The crowd, although militarily alert, issued an involuntary gasp as a caped figure emerged from the portal of the starship. L'Juntara seemed to dwarf even his own troopers as he slowly descended the ramp, his bearded

24

face and the flash of eyes missing nothing in the hangar where he faced his warriors. He returned their salute with a fist that stamped his shoulder and then outstretched in a half-circle before him. His pale, almost colorless eyes scanned the crowd, noting expressions, remembering faces.

One young member of the crowd, supposedly a loyal officer on board L'Juntara's cruiser, shuddered imperceptibly as L'Juntara's pale gray eyes met his, but he held his gaze firm as he watched the leonine head of silver hair disappear. The royal guard cleared a path for their leader as he boarded the lift to the upper levels of the space station.

Lieutenant Altos gave a long sigh of relief, wiping his dark matted hair back from his sweat-drenched brow. How easily his eyes could have given away his cover as an agent within L'Juntarium lines. How easily he could have let his personal hatred flow at the sight of the man who had years before attacked his home world, Aurania, killing most of his own family as well as most of the royal line, and devastating major population centers. How often he had wondered whether it had been his dedication to the Confederacy or his own personal need for revenge that had led him to volunteer for his current position behind enemy lines, isolating himself from family and friends. Now, more than ever, something told him that his sacrifice had not been in vain, for something definitely was happening that could have tragic consequences for the Confederation. No, his own personal revenge must take its place behind his primary function: to discover L'Juntara's plans and how they might affect his home worlds.

The lift carrying L'Juntara and his personal guard reached its final destination and stopped silently, the doors sliding open with a whisper of sound. Surrounded by his guard, L'Juntara stepped out onto the research deck, his entourage following in his wake as he made his way toward the end of a long corridor where a large laboratory, complete with the most advanced technology his scientists could assemble, was located. Entering the stark room, he paused momentarily, then his gray eyes narrowed as they found the glass case containing the turquoise crystal that sparkled with intense light. L'Juntara knew at once that his quest had been a success; the stone was indeed a part of the Exoterra meteor that had streaked into the galaxy from beyond the barrier.

"L'Juntara," one of the priests greeted him, his eyes downcast. But the caped figure walked past him to stand in mesmerized silence before the Exoterra crystal, his gray eyes reflecting all of the fire of the stone.

"You have done well, priest." L'Juntara's voice suddenly boomed across the space between them, releasing the priest from his seemingly petrified stance.

The priest audibly sighed, releasing his pent-up breath as he dared approach L'Juntara. "They have run the stone through computer scanning, and there is no doubt that it is from beyond our galaxy, an element totally alien to our scope of technology. It also meets every description of the so-called Exoterra Stone. In the mind scan we gave to the villager, she revealed the existence of a hooded figure in the swamps of Verdana; a figure that seems to be none other than the rebel scientist, Truestar."

"So Truestar sought Verdana as his sanctuary," L'Juntara said with a gleam of anticipation at the prospect of the capture of the renegade scientist. "If our scientists have not yet found the means to activate the stone, we will surely find out when we capture Truestar."

"I will personally command the mission to Verdana," L'Juntara went on, focusing an adjacent visiscreen on the Verdana system. "We will land on Desera, third moon of the planet, and use that as a base to monitor recovery operations. You priests will pay a prolonged visit to Theos and find out as much as you can about this hooded figure. We may learn Truestar's whereabouts before he discovers our presence on Verdana." L'Juntara continued warningly, scanning each member of his staff, "We do not want the Confederate command on Doros to become suspicious of our movements on Verdana, since it is technically still neutral space. And I do not want any interference from them until I am assured that Truestar is captured and the Exoterra Stone is in my command. And as you know," L'Juntara added, his eyes clouding ominously, "Truestar is sly, as well as desperate. If we attempt an all-out assault, he might escape or be killed at our hands or his own. He will not allow himself to be captured. We can't risk it. He might destroy the Exoterra Stone if he knows how, rather than have us capture it. But now it's only a matter of time," L'Juntara said, gray eyes glowing as brightly as the Exoterra crystal. "With the Exoterra power there will no longer be neutral space, or even a Confederacy. The galaxy will become my empire, and no force known to the rebels will be able to stop me this time." With a wicked smile L'Juntara pronounced this death sentence on the free worlds who would oppose him, his mind reeling with his vision of unrestrained power.

CHAPTER 5

It was quiet in the columned palace grounds as Orion gathered his cape around his tunic and left his quarters for the courtyard below, his destination the edge of the nearby cliff. Prince Orion's features were framed by dark blond hair, and his vivid green eyes gleamed with youth and yet transmitted a certain ageless knowledge far beyond his years. Here he could stare out over his world and view the stars almost within reach above his head. He followed the path that wound away from the courtyard, and soon he was standing on the edge of the escarpment. Since the planet, Aurania, had no moon to dim the intensity of the billions of stars that crowned the heavens, the black sky was filled to bursting with the twinkling lights that Orion knew were actually burning suns.

He lay on his back and stared up at the starlit canopy above his head, the sound of the sea crashing against the rocks below, blotting out the sounds of civilization from the Auranian capital, Altapolis. Here the young prince felt alone with the universe, wondering what was happening on each of those distant worlds. Although his extensive education had included learning of other worlds and techniques of star travel, Orion knew that in many ways his education had been limited by his relative isolation on Aurania. He had seldom in his fifteen years ventured from the surface of his home planet, and then only on brief diplomatic missions at the request of the governing council that would rule Aurania until he came of age. He was painfully aware that in many ways he still had much to learn.

Lost in thought, Orion suddenly became aware of a

presence behind him, and at that exact moment a hand gripped his shoulder with startling strength.

"Alex!" Orion exclaimed delightedly. He sat up and turned to look at the man who had approached so stealthily. He knew well that handsome high-cheekboned countenance framed by dark brown hair and those indigo eyes that twinkled with the same mischievous nature as his gleaming smile. "I didn't expect you to return until tomorrow. How was Govanos?"

"Fine, my young nephew," Alex said as he ruffled Orion's hair and sat down on the grass next to him. His warm regard for his late brother's youngest and only surviving son was obvious. "The trip was very successful. Govanos will be more than eager to buy our surplus crops . . . and the Govanos ladies were as beautiful as ever."

"Some diplomatic mission," Orion teased as he grasped shoulders with his uncle, returning the Auranian sign of affection.

"And just what planet is your mind on tonight, strange one?" Alex remarked with a casual yet guarded tone. It troubled Alex that Orion had not sensed his approach with that strange Aural power of his.

Alex had a vivid recollection of the time as a child in the royal palace on Aurania when he had stood with the rest of the royal family as the newborn son of his late brother, King Jarron, was revealed. All were awed when the baby had gazed up at them with those emerald eyes, the birthmark of those blessed with the gift of the ancient Aura.

Ever since, that period of early history now shadowed in legend, there had been tales of the green-eyed ones, their eye coloring signifying that they had a supernatural interaction with fields of energy and dimensions of nature far beyond the comprehension of the rest of humankind. And now, after many generations, the power of the Aura had shown up again, in the youngest son of the Auranian king.

Alex had foreseen early on that the youth's life

would be far from normal, and therefore fought against the overprotective hand of his brother. In the process, he had befriended his nephew. The camaraderie had helped Orion escape the potential isolation that might have arisen in an effort to protect his unique power.

But Orion's nascent Aural senses had not detected the surprise attack that L'Juntara had launched on the defenseless Aurania several years earlier. Because of a trade disagreement, L'Juntara had deployed his fleet to the peaceful planet. The attack had been brutal, devastating many of Aurania's cities, especially the beautifully columned Altapolis, whose streets were crushed to ruins.

The ancient palace and its occupants were not spared. The royal family, including King Jarron and his beautiful wife, Daras, Orion's brother, Leonis, and sister, Tiana, were slain in the onslaught. Only Orion's protective Aural field had saved him from the falling columns that had crushed the rest of his family.

It was an image that Alex would never forget—Orion, barely alive, buried in smouldering ruins of the once-regal palace, his arms around the crushed body of his brother, Leonis. Thereafter Alex adopted Orion and set about rebuilding their lives. Aurania began the same process of rebuilding after L'Juntara's fleet had been turned back by a joint Confederate effort. After the attack, Alex had insisted that Aurania become a member of the planetary alliance.

Alex met his nephew's intense stare. Sometimes he felt that he would never understand the Aura, this strange power that his nephew possessed that could interact with fields of energy and understanding unimaginable to himself. Yet not for one second did he doubt the efficacy of the ancient gift.

"I guess I'm still thinking about Ambassador Peres's visit to Aurania," Orion explained a trifle lamely, for he had in fact read his uncle's recollections and had been saddened by the memories of the Auranian holocaust.

"I'm sorry that I upset you, Orion," Alex sighed, realizing that Orion had read his mind. "And what news does that pessimist Peres bring to Aurania?" Alex asked curiously, hoping to divert his nephew's train of thought.

"As usual he brings little good news," Orion replied. "L'Juntara is once again up to something. He has left Juntar for the fringes of his empire. I know it has something to do with the discovery of that strange meteor and Truestar's flight. It worries you too, doesn't it Alex?" Orion questioned. "Is there talk of this elsewhere?"

Alex shrugged, brushing a hand through his dark hair. "The usual speculations about Juntar, but nothing more. I had not heard yet of L'Juntara's movements, so for once the diplomats have been able to keep their mouths shut. It is best that there is no talk. There seem to be spies everywhere these days. Remember to guard your tongue, my boy," Alex cautioned him with a smile, but Orion suspected that he was quite serious.

"Even here on Aurania?"

"Everywhere, even with me, perhaps." Alex laughed, making light of his earlier remarks as he saw the look of consternation on his nephew's face. "Oh, I almost forgot, I've brought you a present," he said, adroitly changing the subject as he pulled a bottle from a fold in his cloak. "I was hoping to find you here, for I know of no other place in the universe as lovely as this, where I might enjoy a swallow of this imported nectar. It is genuine Burganberry nectar. Grown only on a very primitive planet in a distant sector, and soon I suspect it will have to be smuggled through Juntarium lines. On Govanos I met up with an old merchant who told me he'd bought the bottle on Juntar in the old-quarter black-market area."

Alex produced two cups from his cloak as deftly as a magician might. "Alex, you've thought of everything. This bottle of nectar has really been around," Orion said approvingly, a gleam of anticipation in his green eyes.

"Not everything," Alex replied in disgust as he struggled with the bottle. "I forgot a corkscrew."

"Leave it to me; it will be my contribution," Orion said. He gestured at the bottle with barely a flick of his hand. There was a popping sound and the cork floated free.

Alex shook his head, feeling once again a sense of awe at his nephew's Aura, even after so many years. It was an awesome gift that even its owner did not totally comprehend or control. "I must convince that stubborn governing council to allow you to accompany me on some of my missions, for you would be a handy fellow to have along in a tight spot," Alex said pensively.

"I wish you could influence them, Alex, for it is a dream of mine to see many other worlds." Orion took a sip of the Burganberry nectar. "I love Aurania, and will always be an Auranian, for I know that I could not live contentedly anywhere else, but . . ." Orion's voice trailed off softly.

"But?" his uncle urged him.

"But I need to learn firsthand about the other peoples and worlds. You understand that, don't you, Alex?" he asked, but it was more a statement of fact than a question.

"Yes, I do," Alex said drily. "But I doubt if other Auranians do," knowing too well how the Auranians guarded their leader and his mystical powers. "Come, now, enjoy your nectar and let us talk of other things. I know you will wish to hear of my travels."

"This is extraordinary nectar," Orion murmured. "I've never tasted anything quite like it before. Why, it's almost like an elixir." Then a wave of dizziness hit him, and the stars began to swirl and blur before his eyes.

Suddenly Alex and Aurania faded into nothingness and he saw two strangely dark eyes staring almost beseechingly at him. Then a hooded figure, an apparition, appeared, blocking out the other as it beckoned to him; then it too vanished.

"Orion, what's wrong?" Alex exclaimed as he put down his glass and put a steadying arm around his swaying nephew's shoulders.

"Alex, I . . . I had the strangest sensation just then," Orion whispered, afraid his spoken words would bring the strange visions back again. "I've never felt quite so adrift and alone before, or quite so terrified of something unknown," he said with a shiver of apprehension.

"It's the Burganberry nectar, I suspect," Alex suggested rather unconvincingly, trying to ease Orion's fear. "It does have a heady effect on those not accustomed to its rare flavor."

"Yes, I suppose so," Orion agreed in a subdued tone of voice, not fully accepting Alex's explanation. Both knew that although Orion's Aural power was unstable, there was always some degree of truth to his visions.

"Come, we should both get some rest this evening. I can see you are still troubled, and I—well"—Alex smiled as he rose and held out a hand to help his nephew to his feet—"I have to meet with the High Council tomorrow and report to them on the most minute details of all my activities, and they expect me to be at my best."

As they walked along the sea cliff, the sound of the surging ocean surf muffled their footsteps. Orion glanced up at the stars and felt none of their usual attraction. Instead he felt an uneasiness as his eyes were drawn away from the familiar star patterns he usually studied and toward a faint twinkling light that was very dim, barely visible, and that he knew lay in a far distant, largely uninhabited sector. With an uncomfortable reluctance, Orion pulled his gaze away from the heavens and stared purposefully ahead of him at the columned palace, rebuilt since the war. He refused, despite the almost overwhelming temptation, to glance once again at that strange distant star. He chided himself for his fanciful imaginings as he entered the palace, passing the grove of ancient cypresses that had survived the war. Their presence eased him somewhat and he allowed the quiet peacefulness of his surroundings to soothe him.

CHAPTER 6

On Desera, a star cruiser came to rest in one of the many craters that pockmarked the desolate surface of the arid moon. Though the atmosphere was thin, it was breathable with occasional aid from a portable oxygen unit. The rust-colored surface of the moon was lifeless now save for the crew of the recently landed large Juntarium starship. In the distance, contrasting sharply with the dead browns and grays of Desera, the surface of Verdana loomed brilliantly green and blue, dwarfing the horizon with its greater size.

On the flagship of L'Juntara no guard had been posted by the main exit portal, and now all was silent on board as the crew slept deeply after the hectic events of the last few days. On the bridge the blinking lights of the life-support system and the communicator gave off an eerie glow, but there was no one there to notice, for if any communication came through or if the automatic sensors detected any movement in the sky above, the computer alarm system would instantly awaken the crew.

From the corridor a young dark-haired crewman quickly approached the portal. He pressed the computer link and said softly, "This is Lieutenant Altos requesting clearance to leave the ship. I require no additional sleep and would like to explore the areas beyond the perimeters of the base."

The computer, recognizing the vocal tones, responded almost instantly. "Lieutenant Altos cleared to leave ship. Portal will remain unlocked until your return."

The hatch slid open with a soft whisper and Altos stepped down onto the dusty terrain of Desera. After hiking across the crater that sheltered the cruiser, he climbed the steep rocky wall up to the rim, taking frequent breaths from his air unit to maintain his strength. He continued walking until he found himself behind a wall of rock, hiding him from any visual contact with his ship.

He knelt down beside a large rounded boulder and pulled his glove from one hand. Quickly he removed the tiny crystal from the ring that adorned his index finger, knowing that the tiny powerful subspace transmitter secured inside had been instantly activated. Realizing that he only had seconds before the power would fade, Altos glanced around nervously, then began to speak. . . .

On the Confederation hub planet, Doros, Counselor Supreme Peres worked steadily at his desk on the seemingly endless paperwork that was an unpleasant but highly necessary part of his position as governor of the Confederation council. As he worked late into the night, he reflected from time to time on recent events. He wondered if his latest journey to Aurania had convinced its peaceful citizens of the ever-present danger that threatened the safety of their beautiful home. Although he couldn't give the Council conclusive evidence that L'Juntara was preparing for further war and attacks, it never hurt to be prepared. He seemed to have found an ally in young prince Orion, and he knew that when Orion filled Alex in, the latter would see things his way, as always. If only he knew more about L'Juntara's recent movements.

After taking a drink of herb stimulant and wiping his hand over his white tresses, Peres was preparing to return to his work when he was abruptly jolted from his thoughts by an electric shock that numbed his entire arm for an instant. Then he registered the source—the receiver ring that was to be used only in time of greatest emergency by his chief agent behind Juntarium lines, Lieutenant Altos. He frantically tore off the crystal on his ring and listened intently.

"Peres . . . L'Juntara has captured a portion of the Exoterra Stone . . . Juntarium troops will soon be search-

ing for Truestar on Verdana, where stone was found . . .
Based on Desera. L'Juntara commands mission . . . One
cruiser . . . my disguise still intact . . . will attempt to
contact Truestar myself but doubt I can do that . . .
Out . . ."

Peres continued to sit, staring down at the now-dull
crystal, which, having completed its one-time function,
faded with the last words of Altos's message. Peres
raised a shaking hand to wipe his sweaty brow. His
worst fears had now been confirmed. If L'Juntara suc-
ceeded in finding Truestar and activating the stone, the
Confederacy was doomed.

He continued to sit there numbly gazing at the disar-
ray of papers filling his desk. Finally he got wearily to
his feet, feeling like an old man as he moved stiffly to
the visiscreen and punched the High Priority Code,
which would link him instantly with the leaders on all
planets of the Confederation. He took a deep breath,
then began. . . .

On Desera the sun began to illuminate the side of
the moon on which Altos stood, dispelling some of the
greenish glare from Verdana. He watched for a moment
as the rocky surface glowed golden in the oncoming
daylight, then he drew the rest of the ring from his finger
and dropped it into the dust, crushing it beneath the
heavy sole of his boot. He leaned against the boulder
for a moment to regain his poise, then started back to
the starship based in the crater.

CHAPTER 7

The citizens of the Dorosian capital city were amazed
at the number of star cruisers that were streaking across
their sky to land in the special spaceport within the command center. Though the skies of Doros, the Confederation hub planet, were usually quite full of merchant
ships, generally the number of official government ships
from members of the Confederacy were few, and
seldom did so many converge on Doros within hours of
each other. A crowd of thousands had gathered to watch
the different delegations arrive in the command center
spaceport. The Dorosians were pressing against the bar-
riers that separated the landing platforms from the rest
of the open area surrounding it.

A surprised murmur spread throughout the crowd as
a sleek golden vessel hovered overhead, then descended
into the port. It was rare indeed to see Auranian ships
landing on Doros, but to have the command flagship arrive was almost beyond belief. And there was no mis-
taking the royal family's ship, its burnished gold color
set it apart from the metallic gray of most of the other
starships. It also bore the distinctive Auranian royal
seal, the triangle of three colors—sky blue blending into
sea green, and a brown the color of the soil—surrounded by a silver-gold Aura radiating from its depths.

After the royal ship had docked, the crowd moved
closer, hoping to catch a glimpse of the two caped
figures who had disembarked from the Auranian flagship
and then disappeared into the underground shuttle that
would whisk them directly to the High Council chambers.

Alex, officially known as Prince Tau-Alexander, High
Ambassador of Aurania, smiled at Orion's wide-eyed

expression at the pomp and ceremony heralding their arrival as they walked down the long corridor facing the double-doored council chambers. Along each side regally uniformed guards stood at attention as the royal party passed and entered the buzzing chambers of the Dorosian command center. It had taken all of Alex's diplomatic persuasion to convince the Auranian ruling council to allow the royal heir, Orion, to attend this urgently called meeting of all Confederation leaders.

The urgent message from Peres had awakened the Auranians in the midst of a peaceful night, and Alex had made preparations to leave for Doros at once. Then on a sudden impulse, he had asked Orion to accompany him. If the situation was indeed as critical as Counselor Peres's message had indicated, then Alex might not return to Aurania immediately, and Orion would be able to report firsthand the results of this strangely foreboding summons from Doros. Who had been more surprised by the Auranian council's capitulation, it was hard to say, for both Alex and Orion had expected to encounter stubborn argument from the ruling group responsible for the heir until he came of age. But after a thoughtful silence, the council had agreed.

In the crowded council chamber, other diplomats from the Confederate planets were milling about as they whispered among themselves and waited impatiently for Counselor Peres and further explanation of his message of alarm.

Each delegation was announced, but when Orion's identity was revealed, there were curious stares by many of the Confederates, especially those from the outlying worlds. Their whispered comments carried to Alex and Orion. They caught the words "mystic prince" and "possessor of strange powers known as the Aura." Orion and Alex exchanged knowing grins, enjoying the slight mystery attached to their figures.

But their smiles quickly faded as a much-harassed-looking Counselor Peres entered the chambers, surrounded by his guard and aides. He stepped onto the platform at the front of the auditorium and signaled for silence, a totally unnecessary gesture, since the crowd had hushed at his entry.

"My friends and fellow Confederates. This is a dark time," he began gravely. "I have called you all here on emergency notice because all of our home worlds face a dire threat." He went on. "We must continue to be a united front or we are all destined to perish under L'Juntara's control."

Counselor Peres's eyes moved around the room as he let his words fully sink in. "The Confederacy is facing its greatest threat, greater even than the horrible last war, from which we are still recovering. The taking of Geometral and the loss of the Exoterra Stone is graver indeed. And now the path of Exoterra has crossed ours, and I am afraid that our fate is endangered by the power of this strange meteor that has come among us."

"But the Stone has disappeared," one of the ambassadors interrupted anxiously. "Everyone says that it must have been destroyed or lost in space with Truestar. Otherwise he would have contacted the Confederacy by now."

"It has not been destroyed, Ambassador Borzaton," Peres informed him reluctantly, "for L'Juntara has a crystal of it and is now searching for the rest of the Exoterra Stone as well as for Truestar, who is rumored to be hiding on Verdana."

The room sounded as if it had lost sudden air pressure as many of the Confederates sucked in their breaths. This startling piece of news was far worse than any of them had imagined, but their hearts grew even heavier when they heard the rest of Peres's news.

"I have received a message from one of our agents within Juntarium lines. He has informed me that L'Juntara himself has launched, and in fact commands, a mission to Verdana to find the rest of the Exoterra Stone, and Truestar as well. I do not need to explain further what this will mean to the Confederation if he is successful. The power of that stone and the capture of Truestar means the end of our freedom, perhaps even our very existence if we should try to resist L'Juntara."

Orion glanced around the room in growing unease at the worried, often terrified, expressions of the ambassadors standing helplessly in the council room. He could sense their fear as he unconsciously absorbed the shimmering vibrations in the chambers.

Orion's green eyes met his uncle's steady gaze, reading in their dark blue depths Alex's growing concern and pessimistic outlook at this news. Orion suddenly shuddered, feeling a slight pain around his eyes as he saw the flash of a spacecraft, then a burning light.

"They are going to suggest that you command a survey mission to Verdana, Alex." Orion spoke strangely, his voice thick and almost indistinct. "They need to know what is really happening there."

Alex stared at Orion's now pale face in surprised disbelief. Then Peres began to speak once again.

"I have decided, as High Council president, to organize a mission of our own to Verdana. The mission will ostensibly be a scientific one, therefore in a small survey craft, the *Piras,* not a war cruiser, and"—he hesitated, looking almost apologetically at the now-stern features of Alex—"if he will agree to our plans, I select Prince Tau-Alexander of Aurania to head the mission, with second-in-command to be the esteemed pilot Commander Stellara, Truestar's intended wife. A half dozen other key personnel will round out the crew."

With this declaration many of the ambassadors nodded their approval and began speaking words of praise for the grave Auranian. Orion stared admiringly at his uncle, this tall dark man with the determined expression and fiery eyes. Alex had always reminded Orion a little bit of his late father. He stood with the same easy pride and grace of movement that had marked King Jarron. Yes, Orion decided, this was his flesh and blood, someone to be proud of, someone who accepted a new challenge and would see it through to the end—regardless of the threat to his own life.

After the formal vote of approval was taken and further discussion had ended, Counselor Peres announced that the assembly was to adjourn and that the mission would get under way immediately.

Orion perfunctorily made his farewells to the diplomats he had met and accompanied Alex from the room to their private quarters, all the while eyeing Alex's silent figure worriedly. "This is to be goodbye for you and me as well, isn't it, Alex?" he asked as his uncle turned to face him in the quiet of their chamber.

"Yes, Orion." Alex confirmed his words. "We will be leaving within the hour. I just wanted a brief moment with you to bid you farewell. I want you to return to Aurania first thing tomorrow. I've left orders with our captain to see that you are sent safely home," Alex explained in a clipped tone of voice, his next words sounding unusually harsh to Orion's sensitive ears. "I won't lie to you, or pretend that this mission will be an easy or safe one. In fact, Orion," Alex added, gazing intently into his nephew's deep-green eyes, "it may be a long while before I see you or Aurania again. If our mission fails and we do not rescue Truestar, then the fate of the Confederacy is doomed. I hope that you will try to explain this to the council. Firm up home defenses and convince them of the need to support any decision Peres makes. You have seen what went on here today and I know you are well aware of the threat that we face. Try to convince the council."

"I have more power over them than they think," Orion said wistfully.

Alex smiled as he hugged his nephew. "I hope you are right, but then, I've always trusted your instincts, strange one," Alex said gruffly as he quickly walked to the door of their chamber. "Farewell, Orion."

"Alex!" Orion called out to him suddenly, a strange look in his eyes as he asked what seemed an irrelevant question. "Where do Burganberries come from?"

"Burganberries?" Alex repeated incredulously. "You want to know where Burganberries come from?" he murmured shaking his head. He frowned for a moment as he thought, then he smiled crookedly as he spoke with

43

understanding. "From Verdana. Strange coincidence, isn't it?" Then he quickly left the room.

Orion continued to stare at the closed door. Coincidence? No, he thought uneasily, there was never anything coincidental about the Aura. But why should he have a vision concerning Verdana and Burganberries? Suddenly he remembered that strange vision on the cliff beside the palace and how his eyes were drawn to that star in that faraway sector. The Verdana system, he knew now, was in that sector. But why should he have a premonition concerning Verdana, unless it had been of what lay in store for his uncle? But he'd seen brown eyes in the Aural vision, and Alex's eyes were dark blue. Orion rubbed his aching temples, the blood seeming to pound in his head. Then the room swirled around him as he fell to his knees and a blackness engulfed him.

Bright, searing light flashed through his mind, stabbing deep behind his eyes. He felt as if he were burning up with fever; then suddenly there was a quiet coolness surrounding him.

He saw the woman, Stellara, then a strange girl peering down at him, but he wasn't afraid of them. The hooded image floated past him again and he strained to see beneath the hood concealing the countenance. A cold sweat broke out on his brow. He had to find out who that hooded figure was. For some unexplained reason the answer seemed vitally important to him. The unmistakable taste of Burganberries was suddenly in his mouth and Orion nearly choked as he gasped for air. Looking up, he saw familiar brown eyes, only this time there was an unfamiliar face attached to them, then it faded in a wave of pain.

When Orion awakened he lay still, his breathing ragged as he stared up at the ceiling. He rose to his feet like a sleepwalker, gathering his small collection of belongings and packing them absently into his bag. Without a backward glance he left the room, his steps carrying him along the now-silent corridors of the administrative complex. He moved like a whisper, seeing no one, a determined expression seeming strange on his

44

usually placid features. He knew what he must do, and there was no turning back for him now.

He assumed he had been unconscious for only a few minutes but it had seemed a lifetime, and in those few lost minutes his destiny had been decided, whether he'd been willing or not.

Before he realized it, he had entered the hangar decks and was quickly coming to the docking area where the *Piras,* the Dorosian survey vessel that had been selected for the Verdana mission, was now being prepared for her journey. Orion stood unobserved in the passageway, his eyes moving quickly over the docking crew, busy at their individual tasks. Then he wandered on to a small group of crewmen standing attentively around Alex and Stellara. Their backs were turned to him, and without further hesitation Orion walked quickly yet purposefully across the hangar deck, his progress unchallenged by anyone. With a sigh of relief, he entered the hatch of the small survey craft. Stopping briefly to get his bearings, he then moved toward the back of the ship, where he guessed the storage section must be. Sliding back a panel, he stared down at the contents of the storage compartment and silently climbed behind the large carton full of supplies that filled the front of the large square space. Closing the panel again, he settled down to wait in the darkness.

CHAPTER 8

"Entering Verdana system. Prepare for transition to sublight speed. Set course for Seahna, second moon," Alex said as he adjusted his controls, the blinking lights casting strange shadows across his stern face.

"Orbit and entry pattern set in," Stellara returned as she watched her flight panel. Then almost reluctantly she let her gaze stray to the surface of Verdana, looming up before them. "I wonder if Truestar could really be there and still alive." She unconsciously spoke her thoughts aloud.

"Well, if he is fortunate enough to be alive," Alex said grimly, noticing his silence was causing more tension than they already felt, "then I hope for all of our sakes that we're the ones to find him."

Alex studied his copilot. He could easily see why Truestar was so fond of her. Her long blond hair and strangely slanted violet eyes were a striking combination that maintained their beauty even though she was well into forty standard cycles. But equally attractive was her sense of loyalty and professional skill that had made her one of the best starship commanders in the Confederation fleet. Originally from Doros, her first marriage had ended abruptly when her husband and young son were slain by creatures, originally thought to be nonliving rocks, while on a survey mission to the galactic hinterlands. After this loss she had devoted her life to space travel, piloting Truestar on many of his scientific missions to uncharted worlds.

In preparation for an imminent landing on Seahna, Stellara turned on her intership scanner, automatically scanning the members of the crew. It was almost in disbelief that she saw the body functions of a *ninth* crew member being registered on her screen. Stellara blinked her eyes, rubbing the weariness from them as she reprogrammed the computer, but once again there was a ninth crew member being registered.

"I suspect we have a stowaway on board, Prince Alex," Stellara said quietly as she pulled her laser from its position at her waist.

"A stowaway? That's impossible."

"The computer doesn't lie, but I've double-checked it for malfunction just to be sure. This is no mistake," she informed him firmly as she stood up and prepared to confront their guest.

"Where is he?" Alex demanded.

"I've registered his life readings coming from a storage compartment in the back of the ship. I think it's about time we had a meeting with our uninvited passenger."

"Do you need any help? Take one of the crew. This intruder could be dangerous—maybe a Juntarium agent," Alex warned.

"I'm used to dealing with miscreants," Stellara reassured him. Then she added, with a glint in her purple eyes, "But I almost hope he will give me trouble if he's indeed a Juntarium spy."

Stellara made her way unaccompanied along the narrow passageway, her almost silent steps carrying her to the darkened area recessed in the rear of the ship. Stellara checked her weapon, setting it on kill, knowing there was seldom a second chance with a Juntarium trooper.

Standing just to the side of the panel, Stellara ordered in a cold voice, "If you value your life, you will climb slowly from the storage compartment. Otherwise I'll blast you out. Come on out; we know you are in there."

Stellara held her breath as she watched the panel slide slowly open as directed. Then, in the darkness, a shadowy form began to emerge, and with a sudden flick of her hand Stellara trained a beam of light from the overhead lighting on the stowaway. Her eyes widened in stunned surprise as she recognized their hidden guest.

"Prince Orion!" she spoke shakily, sighing in nervous relief as she realized how close she'd come to sending the Auranian heir into eternity with her laser.

Orion stood rather sheepishly under the sudden glare of the overhead bright lights shining in his eyes. Putting up a hand to shade his eyes, Orion stared toward the direction of the abrupt summons and the shocked exclamation.

"Commander Stellara, a pleasure," Orion said politely as he caught a glimpse of golden hair, recognizing the Dorosian officer.

"I don't think it will be quite the pleasure you imagine, Prince Orion," Stellara returned angrily as her fear faded and her temper began to take over. "I'm sure your uncle, Prince Alex, will have a *proper* welcome for you. I assume he knew nothing about your presence here on board," she replied with overpolite emphasis, her violet eyes glowing with barely suppressed anger.

Orion didn't need his hypersensitivity to realize that Commander Stellara was slightly put out by his actions in stowing away on board. He eyed her thoughtfully for a moment, debating whether or not an explanation might help, then decided as he saw her set mouth that it wouldn't.

Realizing explanations were useless, Orion sighed. "You'd better take me to Alex. I'd try to explain my presence here, but I doubt if you'd understand, commander."

Stellara's arched brows rose curiously. She had the impression that she'd just been rebuked in some way. With a cool look and condescending nod of her head, she indicated that Orion should follow her. Turning abruptly, she led the way back to the helm of the ship, unaware of Orion's amused grin behind her stiffly held back.

"Our stowaway, Prince Alex," Stellara said with an unconcealed note of enjoyment in her voice as she stepped aside to allow Orion to follow her onto the bridge.

Alex swung around in his chair, his look of curiosity

49

changing to one of disbelief as he stared at his nephew's flushed face. "Orion! In the name of Aranellus, what in blazes are you doing here? By the red suns of Sando, do you know what you've done?" Alex demanded. "We're not on a diplomatic mission to Doros this time, Orion," Alex reprimanded him, then raised his eyebrows heavenward as a new thought hit him. "May Aranellus help me when the Auranian council finds out about this. By now I'm sure they are well aware of your disappearance. Even if I manage to come home from this mission in one piece, I dread setting foot on Aurania."

"Alex, please, I'm sorry, but you don't understand," Orion began, remorse for his actions warring with the certainty of what the Aura had shown him.

"All I understand is that you've placed yourself, and me, in a very difficult and dangerous position. You, the gifted heir to the throne, putting yourself in jeopardy like this," Alex interrupted, not in the mood to hear any excuses for Orion's acting on what seemed an irresponsible whim by a young man intent upon adventure and excitement.

Orion bit his lip, deeply hurt by Alex's refusal to listen to his explanation. He was stunned by the fact that this was the first time either of them had spoken angry words to the other.

"Stellara, take Orion back to the crew quarters and see that he's secured for landing," Alex ordered as he turned back to his control panel. "We will discuss this disobedience of yours later, Orion. There are more important things to take care of right—"

"What is it?" Stellara asked as Alex broke off his sentence abruptly, his narrowed gaze remaining on his scanning screen.

"It's a Juntarium warship, and they were waiting for us on the far side of Seahna, just out of scanner's range," Alex bit out, his blue eyes blazing with a fury Orion had never before seen.

"How did they know?" Stellara cried as she quickly took her copilot's seat.

"The same way we knew about L'Juntara's movements and the discovery of the Exoterra Stone on Verdana. We've fallen into a trap."

"But surely they won't attack; we are still in neutral space," Stellara said worriedly even as she pressed the emergency alarm, sending the ship's personnel into alert status. "Orion, take that auxiliary seat back there."

Orion quickly secured himself and stared out the visiscreen at the curve of Seahna's horizon with the approaching unidentified spaceship.

"We have to try and outrun them until we can make the jump into hyperspace. I'll try to open communication channels with them, if just to keep them from firing on us while you make the necessary calculations," Alex said grimly, then glanced over his shoulder at the pale Orion sitting behind him. He tried to smile reassuringly at his young nephew.

"I'll be all right, Alex, and I'm sorry," Orion said softly.

Alex nodded; then, turning around, opened communications between their ship, the *Piras,* and the Juntarium war vessel. "This is Prince Tau-Alexander of Aurania. This ship is on a Confederation survey mission of this quadrant. Please identify yourself and approach no closer."

The silence on the other end of the communication seemed endless as they anxiously awaited the reply.

"This is Juntarium space. Drop all defense shields and prepare to be boarded. Repeat. Drop all shields or we will open fire."

Alex angrily flipped off the channel and turned to Stellara. "We'll have to get out of the pull of Seahna's gravity before we can attempt the jump, but as soon as we make our move, the warship will be on top of us."

Alex activated the intership intercom. "Within seconds we will be under attack by a Juntarium warship. Prepare for battle."

As the *Piras* moved suddenly away from the orbit of Seahna, the first attack came from the Juntarium ship, its aim faultless as it targeted the engines, each successive jolt weakening the shields protecting the Auranians.

Flashing lights on the flight panels of the *Piras* warned of the overloading of the engines, one having already sustained serious damage. Through the visiscreen Alex could see the surface of Verdana growing larger and larger by the second, and their return fire was easily deflected by the larger warship. Alex suddenly thought of a plan of escape for his nephew. It was risky, but then, he knew that they would never be able to make the transfer to light speed now, not with the damage they had received. Even as he formulated his desperate idea, the last of the shields gave way and an explosion rocked the ship, sending Stellara sprawling to the floor.

"Confederate ship. You have only seconds to surrender. Our scanners show that your ship is severely damaged structurally. We are at this moment locking onto you with our tractor beam. Do not attempt to resist," the cold Juntarium voice droned over the communicator. A shiver of dread went through both Alex and Stellara as they recognized the voice as that of L'Juntara himself, the cold bass tones seeming to seal their fate as the soon-to-be-captured . . . the mission a failure.

Another explosion sent a cloud of smoke boiling into the bridge of the *Piras,* and Alex knew now without any doubt that they had lost. "But I won't let L'Juntara have a total victory," he thought, a determined light in his eye. Quickly he set the controls on automatic and moved away from the flight-control panel. Stellara glanced at him curiously as she struggled to her feet, accepting his hand as she flexed a sore shoulder.

"That last explosion was in the crew members' area; I fear that there are many dead. They don't know that Orion is aboard," Alex began, leading them away from the useless controls and down the narrow corridor. Stellara broke away and disappeared into the crew's quarters, returning a second later with a grim sadness hardening her features.

"I found four dead, the doctor is wounded, and a sixth crewman is in critical condition," Stellara grimly informed him.

Alex swore under his breath as he continued down the corridor, turning into a darkened room of the ship, stepping over rubble and debris as he made his way determinedly to controls set into the wall.

"I don't intend to allow my nephew to die at the hands of a Juntarium warship," Alex promised, as he began to punch out a series of numbers on the control panel.

"What are you planning, Alex?" Stellara demanded as she watched him in growing amazement. "The capsule? You plan to send Orion out in it? Where? To Verdana?" She guessed correctly. "But Alex, he'll never make it. The capsule will burn up when it enters Verdana's gravity. It's not equipped for an atmospheric entry, just for space use."

"Orion is different, Stellara. He'll be able to protect you both with his Aura shield," Alex informed her as he glanced over at his stunned nephew.

"I won't leave you, Alex! No!" he cried as he ran up to Alex and wrapped his arms tightly around his uncle.

"Aura shield?" Stellara questioned. "I've heard of some extrasensory powers that the prince might have, but to think they protect him from a plunge into a gravitational field—well, that I can't believe. And what do you mean that it will protect us both? I'm not going anywhere," Stellara told the glowering Alex emphatically.

"You will both go where you are ordered to go. We're wasting time. Do you want our mission to be a complete failure?" Alex said as he opened the hatch to the capsule. "Just suppose Orion can protect you, and you do reach the planet's surface. You have a chance to warn Truestar. That's more important than being taken prisoner by L'Juntara. Go, Stellara; you've at least got a chance."

Stellara glared at Alex angrily but she knew he was right, and he was her superior. "Very well, Alex, I'll go," she agreed reluctantly.

"Alex," Orion pleaded, "don't send me away. I'm sorry I came. If I weren't here, you could go in my place. I only came because I had a vision. The power

53

of the Aura was too strong for me to resist. You know I wouldn't willfully disobey you."

"I understand, Orion. And now you've got a chance to prove this Aura of yours by saving Stellara and yourself and perhaps our mission as well," Alex told him as he guided him to the mouth of the capsule. Stellara was already aboard and prepared for their brief flight. "And Orion," Alex reassured him, "you know that as commander of the *Piras* I would never leave my ship, not with crew members still on board. So there's no need to blame yourself. Now go, and good luck in completing this mission. I feel sure we will meet up again, in some world, at least." Alex smiled as he hugged Orion, then silently pushed him into the capsule and shut the door on the two reluctant passengers inside.

Securing the air hatch, Alex stepped back and pressed the lever that released the small space capsule and sent it plummeting down to the surface of Verdana. As Alex began to make his way back to the center of the ship, another explosion sent him flying through the air, and then he was engulfed in blackness. . . .

CHAPTER 9

On board the Juntarium warship L'Juntara was co-ordinating the attack, his eyes glowing with satisfaction as the shields of the Dorosian craft buckled and disintegrated beneath the continued bombardment from his ship.

"Commander!" the chief scanning officer cried out. "Someone has attempted escape from the Confederation ship in a capsule."

L'Juntara moved quickly to his side, staring intently at the scanning scope in front of the crewman. "The fools. Don't they know that they will be burned up as they enter Verdana's atmosphere? Forget them. Put the tractor beams on the Dorosian ship and pull her in. I hope that there are survivors, especially this Prince Tau-Alexander. I rather look forward to questioning an Auranian," he said with a cruel smile of anticipation.

"The craft is breaking up. There have been explosions within the ship's hull. We can't hold it much longer; our beam's weakening it too much. I doubt if anyone can survive. Their main life-support systems must have failed by now," the scanning officer informed his superior.

Sitting next to L'Juntara, Lieutenant Altos fought valiantly to control the stab of pain that shot through him as he watched the survey ship being torn apart. How good it had been to hear the familiar voice of his old friend Prince Alex, remembering the days they had spent together at the space academy on Doros. But the voice brought dread as well, for he'd known that there could be no escape for Alex when his ship had flown into the trap set by L'Juntara. He watched in sadness as the capsule that had been ejected from the mother ship sped lower, to its certain fiery death in the skies above Verdana. Who would have attempted such a suicide mission? he wondered in amazement. Only someone who had nothing to lose, he thought with a feeling of growing rage and anger at the injustice of it all. And yet here he sat impotently watching his friends' deaths, unable to raise a hand to help.

"Most of the ship has broken apart; we have only a small piece of it on board, L'Juntara," the helmsman added as he registered the news coming in from the hangar deck.

The crew on the bridge of the Juntarium vessel watched in silence as the Dorosian ship broke apart, some of the sections floating into an orbit of their own around Verdana before they would fall ultimately in a mass of burning metal to the surface.

"So much for the proposed rescue of Truestar," L'Juntara declared as he switched off the visiscreen. "We need not concern ourselves with another Confederation attempt at heroics. By the time they learn of the failure of their mission and the destruction of their ship, we will have found both Truestar and the Exoterra Stone."

Within the small confines of the space capsule that had broken loose from the *Piras,* Orion and Stellara were crouched close together, their knees nearly touching as they stared at each other in silent agony, each feeling the loss of Alex and neither knowing if they themselves would survive the plunge to Verdana.

Stellara was certain that they would not, for she had no faith in the powers of auras or extrasensory perceptions, or anything else that she couldn't track on a computer or flight panel. She felt she should have been allowed to stay on board the *Piras,* where at least she would have died with some semblance of dignity, rather than dying stuffed inside a spinning capsule that would soon turn into a ball of fire. Suddenly she began to feel heat as they entered the atmosphere of Verdana. She was so preoccupied with her thoughts and concerns that she

56

jumped when she felt a hand grasp hers. She glanced over at the other occupant of the capsule, someone she'd forgotten about for a moment, and she was startled by the sudden brightness of Orion's strange green eyes. They seemed to be glowing in the darkness, and despite the intensifying heat, she shivered involuntarily.

"Hold onto me, Stellara," Orion commanded her in a voice that sounded strangely soothing in this moment of terror for them.

At first Stellara thought that the young prince sought the comforting touch of another human being, but soon she found that as his fingers touched her, she felt an extraordinary tingling sensation spreading throughout her, cooling her warm blood, slowing her heart down to its normal rate. She felt that she was slipping into a mesmerizing state of tranquility in which she was completely protected and sheltered from the enormous atmospheric pressures being exerted on their space capsule as it fell to Verdana.

Never before had Orion needed to call upon all of his Aura's strength. Even as a child, when Aurania was attacked, his Aura reacted automatically to save him from the falling palace columns that had slain his family. He didn't know how strong a force he could summon, nor how long he could maintain it. Already he could feel himself weakening, as if he were being drained of his life's blood. His breath was coming in shallow spurts as he trained his mind on protecting the inner layer of the capsule against the encroaching heat that had turned the outer shell into a mass of flames. He must continue; he must hold out long enough for them to reach safety. But already he was feeling a warm flush spreading across his skin. His grip tightened on Stellara's hand, causing both of them excruciating pain. Each seemed to be beyond noticing as Orion made a final effort to strengthen his fading Aura. Gradually he saw Stellara's pale face begin to float before his eyes, until she drifted completely from his sight, and then there was nothing except oblivion before him.

CHAPTER 10

Marseahna rolled over on her side, the stars twinkling down on her through the opened square of her bedroom window as a soft breeze lifted the curtains. She had rushed through her chores earlier than usual that morning, opening the waterwheels that quenched the thirst of her Burganberries during this dry Verdanan season. She had joined the other villagers at noon in following the priests throughout Theos as they inspected every house and shop and outbuilding in search of something they would not reveal. Their questions about strangers and the hooded figure had seemed endless. Later the priests had even visited Marseahna's farm, examining every part of her dwelling and the surrounding fields.

Marseahna flopped back on her feather mattress. It was strange that the priests had come to Verdana, especially since it was not a feast day, which came only with the fullness of Desera, now barely a sliver in the night sky. And yet the priests had arrived on the sands of the Aquagran and were walking through the streets of Theos, asking questions of all citizens.

Marseahna cradled her head with her hands as her eyes were once again drawn to the black sky and stars outside her window, and with a sigh she gave up trying to sleep and stared in fascination at the vista. Suddenly her eyes widened as she saw a flash of light, which seemed to grow steadily brighter. She sat up in bed, her shoulders rigid as the fireball seemed to shoot right past her window. Jumping from her bed she leaned out of the window, just managing to catch a glimpse of the fiery object as it curved downward and fell into the Low Forest, which now emitted a sullen glow of orange.

She remained transfixed at the window for an instant,

then quickly dressed and left the farmhouse. She moved with ease along the familiar paths of the Burganberry fields, her tracks carrying her to the far edge, where without stopping she vaulted easily over the cross-railings of the field fence and moved toward the Low Forest, the faint glimmer of light and hot smell of burning metal guiding her.

Marseahna came to a sudden halt as she entered the clearing where she had expected to see the remains of a star falling. Her mouth dropped open as she stared at the strangely shaped metal object being sucked into the black water of the marsh, the steam rising from it in vapors and hissing like some writhing snake. Marseahna risked moving a step closer, only to stand in shaking, paralyzed fear as part of the blackened metal began to move upward, leaving a gaping hole in the top.

As she watched mutely, a human form emerged, unsteadily and yet with purpose, for it disappeared again and then reappeared, holding another form close to it. As the two shapes perched on the edge of the opening, the capsule bobbed jerkily to one side, dipping down low toward the slimy murk that was steadily pulling it under. Inexplicably Marseahna was no longer afraid, and suddenly her feet were free and she was running toward the object that was beginning to disappear beneath the surface of the marsh. She glanced around frantically, searching for some means of helping the two stranded people. She could see more clearly now that one was a woman, and the other, a slight boy. Marseahna's eyes spotted a fallen log near the edge of the pool, and, testing it for rot, she then rolled it over until she could slide it across the pool to serve as a bridge for the people to climb out on.

"Come on, can you make it?" she cried as they continued to just sit there as if they'd drunk too much.

Summoning up all the courage she had, Marseahna carefully walked across the wobbly makeshift bridge until she stood just below the woman and boy. She could see now that the boy was unconscious, his breathing rapid as his head lolled sideways against the woman's breast. The woman was smaller than she'd first appeared, and could never carry the boy by herself across the narrow log. Her condition was weakened and she had a gash across her forehead, with a nasty-looking bruise already beginning to swell.

"Let me help you, please," Marseahna said to the stunned woman. She held out her arms, begging the woman to look down at her, and suddenly Stellara was able to will herself away from the faintness that had threatened her. She moved Orion closer to Marseahna's outstretched arms while she slid down onto the log, standing next to Marseahna as they maneuvered the inert form of the Prince of Aurania from the burnt-out space capsule.

Moving carefully, they carried Orion to safety just as, with a gurgling noise, the space capsule sank beneath the surface of the stagnant pool, disappearing completely as the murky water closed over it.

Stellara sank down onto her knees in the muddy ground, drained of all power to move now that they had survived such a near-catastrophe. Stellara forced herself to look at the young girl who'd saved them. She tried to clear her thoughts, wondering where her usual quick wits had fled as she tried to place the girl, and, even more important, determine if she was an enemy or a friend.

"My—" she hesitated, unsure for an instant of her story, "—my son and I, we were traveling the swamps in this boat when we—we happened into this bog . . . and our boat was torn by a rock outcropping . . . we were too tired to pull ourselves out, so we must thank you. If you could tell us how to . . ." Stellara's feeble explanation trailed off as she finally gave up fighting off the waves of faintness and fell into unconsciousness at the bemused Marseahna's feet.

CHAPTER 11

At the sudden sound of Stellara's voice, the young girl sitting at the table spun around, nervous curiosity showing openly on her face as she stared at the slender, golden-haired woman. Stellara's purple eyes seemed enormous in her small face as she returned Marseahna's stare unflinchingly, the Verdanan visibly relaxing at the honesty she could read in the other woman's face.

"Please, you will sit with me?" Marseahna invited her shyly. "You will share my food? I will bring you something hot which will make you feel much better," she promised as she rummaged about her heavy pottery jars and carved boxes filled with her precious store of herbs and condiments.

Stellara graciously accepted her offer and sat down in the chair indicated by her hostess. She felt the rough cloth of the long skirt she was wearing, and said with an unaccustomed diffidence, "I put on these clothes I found by the bed; I trust they were meant for me. I could not find my own."

Marseahna placed a steaming cup of some fragrant liquid before Stellara and explained apologetically, "I took away all the clothing you and the boy were wearing and washed it. It was heavy with the scent of smoke. I hope I have not offended you."

Stellara smiled, shaking her head as she saw the worried glance. "No, you have been most kind. I must thank you for saving my life and Orion's."

"Orion? That is your son's name?" Marseahna asked politely. "He is a handsome young man. You must be proud of him."

Stellara looked confused for a moment; then, remembering the lie she had told the girl, nodded in assent.

63

"Yes, he is a most unusual boy, and I am very proud of him." Her own words surprised her as she realized that it was Orion and his Aura that had saved them. They would have been nothing more than charred cinders now if he hadn't been able to protect them. She glanced worriedly at the room where he still lay in a deep sleep and fervently hoped he had not injured himself with his Aural exertion.

"I am Com—Stellara," she stumbled, as she automatically began to state her rank. "As soon as my son is able, we must continue on our way to the mountains, where we must meet a friend."

"Oh, but you must not leave too soon. You are still much too weak. You and Orion are welcome to stay with me for as long as you care to," Marscahna invited her as she caught the look of relief in Stellara's eyes.

"Thank you, but we cannot impose on your hospitality for too long. Besides, we are searching for a friend. Perhaps you have knowledge of him. His name is Truestar."

Marseahna shook her head, "No, I know of no Truestar. He is from the same village as you?"

Stellara paused briefly, then remembered that Verdanans seldom left their home villages. "Yes, we come from the same place. Well, I must check on my son, if you will excuse me now," Stellara began, but was interrupted by Marseahna, who jumped to her feet.

"I will look in on him, if you will allow me," she offered, halfway to the door.

"Thank you. I am still a bit weak, but this herb tea of yours is quite helpful," Stellara complimented Marseahna while pouring herself another cupful of the dark brew.

Marseahna tiptoed closer to the bed, in which the boy, who looked to be about her age, was lying peacefully against the soft quilts and feather pillows. Suddenly the young boy started to talk thickly in his sleep. Perspiration began to drip down his fine features and mat the pale blond hair on his forehead. Marseahna leaned closer as the mutterings became louder and the words more distinct.

"Alex . . . Alex . . . where are you? Alex, I won't leave you. . . . The heat is growing so strong. . . . I can't stand it . . . the Aura . . . I can't hold on any longer . . . it is weakening . . . I can feel the burning . . . we will die."

At the last anguished word, he seemed to awaken with a jolt, clutching the unfamiliar blankets around him almost protectively. He sighed deeply, and gradually became aware of his strange surroundings, realizing he was not in his own bed on Aurania. He opened his eyes and stared disbelievingly at the beamed ceiling above his head, then around at the four white-stuccoed walls of the small room. He noticed with a start the figure standing just beside the bed and staring in fascination at him. His green eyes met the brown ones of the dark-tressed girl, and for a moment they seemed familiar to him, as if he knew this girl, and yet he'd never set eyes on her before.

"I'm Marseahna, and I know that you are called Orion," the girl introduced herself with a friendly grin. "Your mother, Stellara, is in the kitchen."

"She is alive! She is well?" Orion cried excitedly as he started to climb from the bed.

Orion glanced down at his bare chest, his face flushing as he realized his state of undress. Then he looked up at this strange girl and caught the laughter in her eyes and relaxed. "My clothes?"

"Being thoroughly soaked in a cleansing fluid. Here are some that I had here; I hope they will fit and you will not mind wearing them," Marseahna offered, then added hesitantly, "They are not as fine as yours."

Orion smiled as he accepted the tunic and breeches. "As long as they will cover me decently, they'll be fine. Thank you."

Marseahna's smile widened. The clothes had once belonged to a brother who had died in the same plague that had killed her parents long ago, and these had been his best pair of breeches and tunic.

"Your mother and I will be in the kitchen, so when

you are dressed, if you wish to join us, I will have some dinner ready for you. You must be starved." She turned and left, allowing Orion to get dressed.

Orion stood silently staring about him at the crude furniture of the room, comparing the elegant furnishings of the royal palace on Aurania with this rough farmhouse. But there was a certain charm to the plain whitewashed walls of the bedroom, and it was clean, Orion thought as he quickly slipped into the borrowed clothes. He caught a glimpse of himself in a mirror that hung in a plain wooden frame on the wall; and as he moved closer, he could see the strain that still tightened his lips, and the slight shadows beneath his eyes which made the green of them seem even brighter. There was a new and strange look in them. A look of sadness and grief, something that Orion had not experienced since the holocaust. Alex was dead, and he and Stellara were stranded on this primitive planet with this young girl.

CHAPTER 12

They were almost finished with the meal, sitting in the cool shadows of Marseahna's herb garden and sipping their glasses of Burganberry nectar. Orion suddenly remembered the last time he had tasted Burganberry nectar, and the strange vision he'd had. He glanced into Marseahna's friendly brown eyes, seeing them almost for the first time. No wonder they had seemed so familiar, Orion thought in a growing wave of excitement. He had seen those same brown eyes in his vision. Everything he had seen had been part of the future, even to their crashing on Verdana, as well as his stowing on board the *Piras*. It was all meant to be from the very beginning. But there was still something else. What was it he had seen?

With growing frustration Orion was aware of the fact that his Aura powers had been severely weakened by the plunge through the skies of Verdana. If only now he could have a vision that would clarify things. Orion's head ached as he tried in vain to summon his Aura power. Finally he got a glimpse of something more.

"A hooded figure, that was it," Orion said, not realizing he'd spoken aloud until he became aware of the sudden silence and the strange looks on Stellara's and Marseahna's faces.

"A hooded figure," Marseahna said quietly, a frown marring her brow. "The only hooded figures we have seen, Orion," Marseahna explained, not seeing the interested expression on Stellara's taut face, "are the priests of the god L'Juntara."

Stellara shivered at the mention of the dictator and then sighed with disappointment. She had thought to learn something of Truestar.

"They come in a sleek silver ship from out of the skies," Marseahna continued, recapturing Stellara's wandering attention with her next statement. "They always come in pairs, so I do not think one of them would be the hooded figure you speak of. Besides, until recently they have never ventured far from their ship. But now they are walking among us," Marseahna added, glancing over her shoulder almost apprehensively in case one of the tall robed figures had sneaked up behind her.

Stellara and Orion exchanged knowing glances, wondering how long their presence could go undetected. "These priests, they have come to your farm?" Stellara asked, feigning casual interest.

"Why, yes, just yesterday. They wanted to see my fields and my cottage. They asked a lot of questions about a hooded figure too," she added, with a curious glance at her two guests. "But that couldn't be the hooded figure you were asking about, because the priests consider him evil. At least, that's the feeling I get from them."

"Then maybe there is another hooded figure," Stellara continued gently probing.

"Yes," Marseahna confided eagerly. "The one I saw. It was where I found the beautiful turquoise stone. And that is why the priests are walking among us, because of my gift to them."

Stellara swallowed the lump that was forming in her throat. The Exoterra Stone really was hidden on Verdana, and Truestar must still be alive. They might have a chance to find him after all, but they would have to be very careful and not draw attention to themselves. The people of Theos and the surrounding farms seemed to live in a very isolated and insulated society, where a stranger would attract considerable attention and speculation.

"But tell us more about this strange stone you found. Where did you say you found it?" Stellara asked quickly.

"In the swamps. I don't like to admit it, but I nearly died of fright when I saw the figure coming out of the dawn mists. The stone was so beautiful. I've never seen the Aquagran as blue as that stone. It glowed with such light I felt nearly blinded, as if I'd been staring at a sun."

"Do you think you might show us where this happened?" Stellara asked, barely able to contain her impatience.

"I guess that I could . . ." Marseahna began, then spotted a group of figures hurrying across the fields directly toward the large Oakcorn tree under which they were sitting.

Orion and Stellara exchanged worried glances as they watched the figures getting closer.

"Who are they, Marseahna?" Orion asked curiously, eyeing with distrust the half dozen humans astride some form of animal much like the Horistas of his native Aurania. But of course, the peaceful Auranians would never subjugate another living creature by making it a beast of burden.

"They are Vagaso. They have no permanent homes. Villagers and farmers bribe them with food to save their property. Word came just recently to Theos that a nearby village had refused them and it was nearly completely destroyed by them."

Stellara interrupted quickly. "Will they mean us any harm?"

"I don't think you need to fret," Marseahna said soothingly. "They just want some nectar. I give them that and they leave me alone. Now, I want both of you to stay here," she added, grasping a bundle of bottles at her feet. "I had these ready in case they showed up today. I will go meet them. There's no need for you two to get up," Marseahna said reassuringly as she headed off to meet the newcomers.

Orion watched with Stellara as Marseahna ran out to greet the Vagaso. "Much like the Mercai of space. Vagabonds. And they are going to tell the priests about us," Orion said as his tone of voice grew more serious.

"What!" Stellara exclaimed, staring incredulously at Orion, yet accepting that what he said was true. She knew by now not to doubt the young prince's statements, as unfounded as they might seem at the time.

"Yes, they are curious about us and Marseahna is trying to stall their questions or their coming any closer to us. But their next stop is Theos, and the priests will question them. Even they fear the priests."

"Then we must get Marseahna to show us where she found the Stone. That is a starting point," Stellara said, resolutely, her calm commander's voice taking over. "That will give us a start in finding Truestar."

"Yes," Orion agreed. "That is a starting point."

CHAPTER 13

The shadows of the overhanging boughs surrounded them as they entered the Low Forest, picking their way carefully along the treacherous, sometimes hidden pathways twisting through it. As Orion moved deeper into the lush and overgrown vegetation of the marsh, he felt an overwhelming sadness come over him. His mind stretched into space and his last memory of Alex. He had so unselfishly given his life for Stellara and Orion that Orion vowed to finish successfully his uncle's mission.

"This is the place." Marseahna's self-assured words brought Orion back from his wanderings. He refocused his eyes on Marseahna and Stellara standing uneasily by a dark pool of stagnant water. "It was here that I found the stone, but now I see only gray pebbles," Marseahna sighed. She kicked at the underbrush around her, wondering why she had so suddenly trusted these two strangers by showing them the place where she had found the turquoise fragment. But some inner instinct told her she could trust them. If only she could now find another torquoise fragment rather than just common swamp rock.

Orion turned away and stared down into the murky pool of water. He saw his reflection and that of the two women. As Marseahna casually tossed a pebble into the pool, ripples spread out from the center, widening as they reached the banks and disturbing the serenity of the pool and Orion's reflection. Suddenly the ripples started to swirl faster and faster as Orion continued to stare in hypnotized fascination at the uneasy surface. All at once he saw a strange blue glow and that familiar yet unfamiliar hooded figure of his previous vision. A

71

mountain peak seemed to loom above him as he felt himself swaying; then suddenly, when he thought he would fall into the black depths of the pool, a hand gripped his arm hard and pulled him back from the edge.

"Are you all right, Orion?" Marseahna asked in concern, her expression worried as she stared at this new friend's pale face.

"Yes, yes, I'm fine now," Orion whispered. "I'm still a bit tired from the traveling, I guess. Marseahna, maybe you could show us the route through the swamps to the mountains," Orion asked hopefully. Time was of the essence, now that he knew where Truestar was; and unless his vision had misguided him, the rebel scientist was hiding out in the mountain range nearby.

Stellara's eyes brightened visibly at Orion's confident-sounding voice. "Yes, of course, we certainly mustn't overstay our welcome, or bring trouble to you." Stellara said as she turned to Marseahna, who had suddenly stopped dead in her tracks at this latest suggestion from her new friends.

"But you are not rested enough. You have both been through so much," Marseahna argued. "You must at least stay until the morning," Marseahna almost pleaded. And then suddenly, as if to change the subject, she cried, "Look a Dalmara bloom!" She made her way unerringly to a secluded spot nearby where a delicate violet-hued flower blossomed. "They're so rare; so seldom do you find one in bloom. The flower will wilt after only one day unless you pick it. Then it will last for several days, and later the petals can be used in the most exotic perfume," she confided as she bent over and carefully plucked the tender bloom, cradling it almost lovingly in her hand as she started to rise.

A strong wind had risen as Orion and Stellara stood waiting for Marseahna to rejoin them on the pathway. Soon a sudden cracking noise shattered the silence. Looking upward, they saw a large limb splitting wide open and about to fall. Marseahna glanced up in time to see the heavy branch come falling out of the tree directly above her head. She stood frozen to the spot, unable to move as she stared up at the broken limb plummeting down on top of her.

Stellara cried out a useless warning but miraculously the dangerous branch seemed almost to stop in midair, hovering over the Verdanan girl's head before falling harmlessly just to her side, where it crumbled into tiny splinters of wood.

Marseahna glanced over at the others in amazement, expecting to see the same incredulous look mirrored on their faces. But they seemed merely relieved, and not that surprised at what they had just witnessed. Marseahna's mouth dropped open as she stared at Orion's odd-colored eyes, which now glowed with a fire reminiscent of the turquoise stone she had found.

"Are you all right, my friend?" Orion asked in concern. "That certainly was a stroke of luck. If that wind hadn't changed direction all of a sudden, well, I hate to think what would have happened to you beneath that limb," Orion said, purposely making light of the incident as he gradually became aware of Stellara's uneasy presence by his side.

"But the wind is still blowing in the same direction as before," Marseahna commented with a strange look at Orion.

"No matter. As long as nothing happened to you."

"Come on, we'd better hurry on our way toward the mountains," Stellara interceded. "Please show us the way, Marseahna."

For the first few miles Marseahna led the way easily, by recognizing landmarks along the way. But an hour later her pace had slowed considerably as she carefully searched her way among the unfamiliar swamplands. The coming darkness made their progress even slower and more arduous.

Orion glanced around him as he heard the whisperings and scamperings of the small swamp creatures seeking shelter for the night. Birds called out sharply as the trio moved beneath the trees, their passage being marked by the swampland inhabitants. Stellara grimaced as she felt her foot slip into a deep hole of mud, and controlling her involuntary shudder, she eased it out and continued on, trying to forget what slimy creatures might be clinging to her legs.

"This is where I leave you," Marseahna suddenly said, for she had never traveled farther along the path. Her voice was startling to both Orion and Stellara, who'd grown used to the enforced silence of their trek.

"Thank you, Marseahna," Orion said softly as he grasped his new friend's shoulders in the old Auranian way. "You have become a friend in the short time that we have known each other, and I will always be grateful to you."

Marseahna managed to smile awkwardly, knowing she would miss this boy with the pale hair and green eyes that saw so much. "I call you friends as well, Orion and Stellara. Maybe we will meet again. There is a pass in that direction and a way through the mountains. I hope you can locate your friend there," Marseahna said sadly, unhappy at losing her new friends. "I'm sorry that I can't go any farther, but I would never find my own way back."

"You're indeed a good friend," Stellara said fondly, watching as Orion embraced Marseahna warmly. "You've given us more than we could ask. Goodbye, Marseahna."

"Goodbye, my friends," Marseahna said sadly, then she turned abruptly and disappeared back into the shadows of the swamp.

"We must continue now, wherever we are bound," Stellara said, breaking the silence as she glanced over at Orion's averted profile. "What exactly did you see in that vision of yours, Orion?"

Orion shook his head. "Not much, I'm afraid. I saw a hooded figure, the same one I'd seen previously, and then the mountains. It must surely have been a sign to come in this direction."

Stellara shrugged, disappointed that he couldn't be any clearer than that. "Well, it's better than nothing, or better than waiting for Juntarium *priests* to come and find us."

"I think you'd give them a fight, Stellara," Orion said with a grin. He was coming to understand why this woman of Doros was so implicitly trusted by Alex.

"And you as well, my young prince," Stellara complimented him, as she turned to begin the steep climb through the tall pines towering above them.

Orion's tunic caught on a branch. He shook his head in dismay and disbelief. "A few days ago I would have never in my wildest Aura dreams seen myself dressed like this, wearing a rough woolen tunic, instead of my—" Orion suddenly broke off. He and Stellara had the same horrible thought as they glanced down at the clothes they were wearing.

"We left our clothes behind at the farmhouse," Stellara whispered. "How could I have been such a forgetful fool! My uniform is there in plain sight, for anyone to see, including my rank and my order." Stellara cursed herself angrily beneath her breath. When she looked at the silent prince, she was startled. His eyes had a glazed look which she knew by now meant he was having a vision.

"The priests! They've found our clothes. I can see torches lighting up the sky around the farm, and a crowd of people. Fear and superstition are growing like a disease among them." Orion spoke in a hoarse voice full of anguish. "They've pulled Marseahna from the house, dragging her out into the yard and trampling her garden. She's crying. They're questioning her. They want to know why she lied, why she gave shelter to strangers and then hid their clothes."

"You must go on, Stellara." Orion spoke firmly. "They are taking Marseahna to their ship for mind-control questioning. That could destroy her mind. You go on, Stellara. Find Truestar. I must go and help Marseahna if I can," Orion commanded as he began to retrace his steps through the swamps. "I'll try to join you with Marseahna later."

"Orion!" Stellara cried out as she hurried after him.

"Don't go! It won't do any good. How can you get back through the bogs without a guide?" she demanded, trying frantically to reason with him.

Stellara could see his wry smile in the growing darkness as he answered her softly. "I have the Aura, remember." Then he was gone and Stellara was left alone under the pines.

"The Aura," Stellara said dully. "A day ago I scoffed at the very idea, but now"—she paused uncertainly as she looked at the empty clearing—"now I'm willing to believe in anything." She hurried across the clearing, and accidentally stumbled in a hole. Involuntarily she cried out. Her voice echoed off the nearby mountains.

"Who's there?" came the reply in an unmistakable voice.

Stellara's words caught in her throat as she sucked in her breath in surprise.

"Truestar!" she cried. Jumping to her feet, she hurried to the approaching hooded figure, shadowed in the moonlight. "You're alive and I've found you at last," she cried as she embraced him. Relief and joy flooded over her.

Truestar smiled beneath his hood. "Stellara, my love," he said fondly, feeling disbelief as well at seeing her there. "This is not the way that I expected to find the imperturbable Commander Stellara Raschtam-ti-Halla of Doros, stumbling across this godforsaken planet. Are you all right?" he added gently as he looked closely into her strained face and held her tightly to him.

"I'm not sure, although things are definitely looking better now that you're here. Orion and I—"

"Who?" Truestar asked as he looked around the empty clearing. "Is there someone else here with you?"

"I came to Verdana with Prince Orion of Aurania," Stellara told him quietly.

"The Auranian heir?" Truestar allowed his surprise to show. "This is indeed a strange night," he said as he held Stellara closer. "By any chance were you and the young prince in that capsule that fell to Verdana last

76

night?" Stellara nodded mutely, not wanting to remember her too-recent escape from danger.

"I observed that fiery descent, my dear Stellara. You were most fortunate in your selection of a crew member. Now I know why you weren't burned to a crisp when you went through the atmosphere of Verdana. The Aura, of course. I am surprised to find the young heir so far out in space," Truestar remarked curiously. "But where is Orion now?"

"He's gone, Truestar. Gone to rescue a young girl who helped us. Truestar, let me fill you in on what has happened and what brought us here. But first I have some bad news." She hesitated, knowing her next statement would come as a shock to the scientist. "Alex is dead. He was in charge of our mission, and that is why the young prince is with us. But I'll tell you about it as we walk. I don't need his Aura to know that he is in danger now. Truestar, L'Juntara knows that you are here, and he has found a crystal of the Exoterra Stone. His troopers are in the village now. That is the trap that Orion is walking into."

"So that one lost crystal has fallen into L'Juntara's hands," Truestar said softly, his mind traveling back to the day he had landed on Verdana. "Yes, Orion is in grave danger. He may try to overextend the use of his Aura, and risk his own life. We must go at once to the Aquagran." Truestar sighed as he took Stellara's hand and they headed back through the swamplands.

CHAPTER 14

"Priests of Juntar!" Orion called out a challenge as he pushed through the crowd of curious villagers, his eyes seeming to flash a green fire as they caught sight of the Vagaso who had mingled with the citizens to watch what was about to happen to Marseahna.

At such an imperious summons, the priests hesitated on the ramp of their shuttle craft and turned in surprise, the shaking Marseahna dangling helplessly between them.

"Who dares to call on the priests?" one priest demanded as he hurriedly scanned the crowd of villagers. Then his gaze fell on the young man striding boldly through the group, and he nearly released his grip on Marseahna when he recognized the stranger.

Only hours ago they had received a message from L'Juntara that the Auranian heir was missing and thought to have been aboard the survey vessel destroyed above Verdana. And now here was Prince Orion. By some miracle he had escaped the attack.

The priest glanced at the other priest, who had automatically drawn his laser weapon.

"Don't kill him," he warned.

"Don't worry," the comrade assured him. "I'll only stun him if he approaches any closer. What difference does it make what happens to this villager?"

"Fool!" the priest hissed. "He is the Auranian heir. Somehow he has landed on Verdana. One of the uniforms we found at the farmhouse would be his."

"Then he will be armed," the other priest said with sharper interest, raising his laser defensively toward the approaching stranger.

"Will the *priests* consider exchanging their prisoner

79

for me?" Orion demanded as he came to a halt at the bottom of the ramp.

"We do not bargain with Confederates," the priest answered shortly.

"I see that you found my clothes at the farmhouse. Even Juntarium officers can recognize *that* uniform."

"We'll stop those snide remarks soon enough, rebel," the priest spat out angrily.

"Orion, please run!" Marseahna yelled as she struggled with renewed vigor against her captors. "Run, ru—"

Her words were cut off as the priest knocked her nearly senseless with the back of his hand. Then, before the other priest could stop him, he fired his laser at Orion. But the energy ray was deflected and in a split second came back at him. His look of astonishment faded into blankness as he loosened his hold on Marseahna and fell in a heap to the bottom of the ramp.

"Fool!" the other priest cried as he frantically reached for his own weapon and tried to hold onto Marseahna. She was now struggling fiercely to pull her arm loose from her captor's grip. "Prince Orion, the mystic prince. I had forgotton they say you have strange powers. But this girl has no such protection. Will you be the cause of her death?" he threatened, drawing his laser.

But the priest had underestimated Marseahna's strength, and at that moment, with a final desperate lunge she pulled free and raced down the ramp toward Orion.

"Get behind me, quickly," Orion called as the priest swung around, his laser aimed directly at them.

Marseahna slipped behind Orion just as a beam of bluish-white energy hit the prince. But it was as if the beam had come into contact with a solid wall. The priest now took cover behind the edge of the ramp, avoiding the deflected energy.

Since more of his Aura strength was required to send laser beams back rather than merely to stop them, Orion didn't know how long he could hold out against been subjected to such a crucial test of his Aura powers, and he remembered worriedly how the strain of protecting Stellara and himself in the space capsule had left him drained and defenseless.

At the first laser blast and flash of light, the villagers of Theos had disappeared quickly. The beach was deserted except for the four figures grouped randomly around the base of the shuttle craft's ramp.

Orion could feel the sweat begin to drip from his brow as his Aura power shielding both Marseahna and him from the laser started to fade. Orion's legs began to tremble slightly as he felt a growing heaviness against his chest, a sure sign that the force of the laser was beginning to penetrate his Aura field.

"Marseahna," he mumbled. "You must try and slip away. I can't hold out against the continued energy of his weapon. You must get away," Orion told her. "It's me they want. There's no sense in us both being taken prisoner. Go, Marseahna. Please, for me."

Marseahna was kneeling in almost a praying position behind Orion's back, her mind numbed from what she was witnessing. She feared for the safety of her new friend at the hands of the priests, emissaries of a supposed god.

"I'll run to the side and distract him," Marseahna said impetuously. On shaking legs, she tried to run off to the side and draw the fire of the priest.

"Marseahna! Don't!" Orion called out a warning too late. The priest had aimed quickly and accurately and cut down the young girl in her tracks. Before Orion could turn, the wounded priest behind him had come back to consciousness and fired on the unprotected prince, knocking him senseless to the sand.

"I'll have your hide if you've harmed the prince," reprimanded the older priest.

"W-what?" the younger priest mumbled as he struggled to his feet. But before he could get any farther than his knees, another energy beam struck him full in the chest and knocked his legs right out from under him. Once again he fell back onto the sand, unconscious.

81

The head priest turned around abruptly to see a tall hooded figure striding toward him, and a small woman he instantly recognized as Commander Stellara Raschtam-ti-Halla. He was accustomed to seeing her face flashed on their computer screens as one of the top Confederate officers. But his look of recognition was cut short as he was struck by another laser beam. With an almost ludicrous expression on his face, he fell into the sands of the Verdanan sea, his hood falling completely over his face.

"Prince Orion," Truestar said softly as he looked down at the unconscious form of the youngest and only surviving heir of his late friend, King Jarron. "I had not thought to meet up with you again in circumstances so alien to your realm, my son."

"Is he all right?" Stellara demanded, her voice filled with concern. "He looks pale, almost transparent."

"It's his Aura." Truestar said calmly as he placed a hand over Orion's brow. "It can drain him almost completely of all life signs. Until he learns to control his Aura, he may endanger his own safety," Truestar explained, his unworried tone relieving some of Stellara's doubts. "How is the village girl?"

"Just stunned," Stellara told him. "She's even coming out of it now."

Marseahna gazed up into Stellara's purple eyes and felt her head swimming. Dizzily she tried to sit up, and was relieved when she felt a firm hand helping her to her feet. Looking up gratefully, she suddenly sucked in her breath when she found herself staring at another hooded figure. Stellara's slightly smiling face beside that figure was somewhat reassuring. She slid her arm behind Marseahna's waist and helped to support her.

"This is Truestar, Marseahna," Stellara explained quickly as they made their way back to Orion's prone figure. "He is our friend, the one we were searching for. You must come with us now, before these two come back to their senses," she said with a contemptuous glance at the two priests, who were still sprawled on the sand.

Truestar bent down and picked up the still figure of Orion, carrying his slight body easily in his strong arms. "We must go now. We've a long way to travel before Verdana's sun lightens the skies. We must be far away from here by then, and safely under the cover of the high forests." Truestar turned toward Marseahna. "I think it best you come with us until this trouble is over," he said sadly, glancing at Stellara to confirm his feelings.

"Yes, you must go with us, Marseahna. Verdana is not safe for you now," Stellara said, placing her arm around the young girl.

"Thank you," Marseahna mumbled thickly as she dragged her feet slowly through the sand, stumbling now and again from the effects of the stunning ray. "I guess I have angered the god L'Juntara," Marseahna added shakily.

"Yes," Truestar said wearily, stopping briefly to shift Orion's weight in his arms. "We have all angered the *god.*"

CHAPTER 15

Deep within the caverns of the mountains towering above Theos, Orion awakened from his drug-like slumber. His eyelids felt heavy as he tried to open them. He glanced curiously around the rock walls of the chamber, his keen eyes noting that the cavern's symmetry clearly indicated it had been man-made.

In the unnatural light of the cavern it was hard to tell night from day, but Orion sensed that he must have slept through the night and into the day. Suddenly his green eyes widened with remembered fear as he recalled the battle with the priests on the shores of the Aquagran. Marseahna? Where was his friend? Was she even alive? And where was this strange cavern?

Oddly enough, he felt completely relaxed. His heightened Aura senses felt no danger. But the last thing he remembered was being stunned by one of the Juntarium troopers. What had happened that he should now *not* find himself a prisoner of L'Juntara?

"Orion?" a voice inquired softly from a dimly lit doorway.

"Stellara!" Orion cried out in relief and happiness. "I should have known that you'd manage to rescue us," he said as he gave her an impulsive hug. His genuine concern and apparent affection for her caught her off guard for a moment and she hugged him back.

"You gave us quite a scare, young man," Stellara scolded him gently.

"Us?" Orion questioned.

"Yes, us," Stellara informed him with an expression on her face that he'd not seen before. "And if you care to join us, you might learn a few things," she added teasingly, then paused as she looked seriously into his face. "You do feel all right?"

Orion nodded his pale head without hesitation. "I'm fine, Stellara. I'm just not accustomed to using my Aura so intensely. Now you must tell me what has happened. How did you find us, and is Marseahna all right? I saw her fall as I tried to deflect the laser beam," Orion added, his voice filled with worry.

"She is just fine, still a bit stunned and confused, perhaps, but physically she is healthier than you at this minute," Stellara reassured the young Auranian. "Now come and see for yourself."

Orion readily followed her through a narrow passageway into a cavern larger than the one he'd awakened in. He looked around eagerly, his eyes widening in a surge of excitement as he recognized the tall thin man standing with Marseahna, his sensitive hands gesturing in a familiar manner as he explained something to the frowning Verdanan.

"Truestar!" Orion called out as he ran to the side of the legendary scientist.

"Prince Orion," Truestar said with a fond smile, inwardly remarking how the young prince had matured since the last time they had met on Aurania. "I am pleased to see you, my young friend," he said, and grasped his shoulders in the traditional Auranian greeting. "But I would prefer that we were saying hello on Aurania. How I long to see your beautiful palace. I have heard that it is even more beautiful now than before the war. I remember you as a child, swimming like a fish in those sparkling palace pools amid the ancient cypresses. And your beautiful golden-haired mother. And your father, so regal and yet so kind." He sighed with nostalgia; then, collecting himself, he smiled apologetically. "Forgive me, Orion; I didn't mean to remind you of those times so long ago. But seeing you standing there reminded me of that much happier time," Truestar added softly, gazing intently into the eyes of the prince.

"No, please, Truestar"—Orion rushed to speak—

"it gives me pleasure to hear Aurania and my family spoken of so lovingly."

Orion turned to Marseahna, who'd been quietly listening to the exchange. Her eyes were wide with all she had seen and heard since traveling to the mountain caverns beneath Tor Cloudtopt. She was in awe of her friend, this Prince Orion. His courage and powers against the priests had amazed her beyond belief, and now those mystical green eyes were staring into hers. Marseahna felt suddenly ill at ease, as if she should be kneeling before Orion.

Orion could sense the conflict of emotions within Marseahna, and with a calming smile he reached out and held her gently to him for a moment, trying to reassure the young Verdanan that he was still the same person as before.

Marseahna smiled sheepishly. "It will take some time to get used to all these changes," Marseahna explained awkwardly, but her dark eyes shone with the adventure of it all. Most difficult for Marseahna to accept was the idea that the priests were really soldiers of the dictator, L'Juntara, who in fact was not a god at all and meant harm to her new friends and to Verdana. Truestar's words had puzzled Marseahna at first. But then she remembered the village Elder of many years ago who had tried to dominate Theos by laying down arbitrary laws that benefited his own establishment, and deceiving the people into following his wishes. Eventually the villagers rebelled and sent the tyrant from Theos, and he was never heard of again. Apparently this L'Juntara was the same kind of man as the Elder, and must ultimately be overthrown. As she mulled these startling ideas over, her three friends were talking quietly among themselves, their tones sounding anxious and urgent as they watched a strange screen with steadily moving lights blinking rapidly off and on.

"It is as I feared," Truestar stated matter-of-factly, but there was a deep note of worry to his casual remark as he gestured at the screen. "The village of Theos is crawling with Juntarium troopers. I can pick up the readings of their communicators, and there are several shuttles circling this area, as well as the star cruiser of L'Juntara orbiting Verdana," Truestar said grimly. Then, looking at Stellara and Orion, he added, "I'm afraid this planet can no longer serve as a safe haven. We will have to flee before L'Juntara sends more troops."

"But how can we? L'Juntara's warship can outrace us. Now that he knows for certain that you are alive and on Verdana, he will stop at nothing to get his hands on you, Truestar," Stellara warned him. "Our best chance is to stay hidden—much as I dislike the idea of holing up here, when I know I could be doing something more useful for the cause elsewhere," Stellara said impatiently. "If we monitor our energy output very carefully, I doubt L'Juntara's scanners can pick us up in here," she added decisively.

"No, my dear," Truestar said softly, understanding her desire for action. He too longed to be doing something useful once again, but knew that a false move now could endanger the entire Confederacy. "We will not be hunted down here on Verdana. We can escape," he added with a secret smile. "You forget I know how to activate the secret powers of the Stone. With its force there is no ship in L'Juntara's fleet that can catch us. The only problem," Truestar said with a troubled frown, "is what to do with the rest of the Exoterra Stone."

"What do you mean? Isn't it here?" Stellara demanded, looking around as if she expected it to materialize before her very eyes.

Truestar shook his silvery head. "No, it is in the swamp. In fact, it is very near the place where Marseahna found one of the crystals that fractured during its descent into the swamp pool. I put it there, just in case my location was discovered. That way, at least the large stone would be safe. It is the best place to hide it. Deep within a pool of murky water in that overgrown bog of a swamp it is untraceable by the usual scanning devices. In fact, only another scanner boosted by Exoterra power could detect it."

"Couldn't we retrieve it?" Orion asked.

"With a whole regiment of Juntarium troops scouring the Low Forest?" Stellara commented doubtfully. "No, Truestar is right," she added firmly, albeit uneasily. "I think it's safer to just let it remain there for the time being."

Marseahna had been listening intently to the conversation; and now, as the importance of the Exoterra Stone became clear to her, tears began to form in her eyes. It had been her gift to the priests that had put them all in this danger. Suddenly she noticed that they had broken off their conversation and had turned toward her.

Sensing the cause of her unhappiness, Truestar approached her, his smile easing her concern somewhat. "My child," he said softly, his own eyes brimming with emotion, "don't think for a minute we blame you. It is only because of L'Juntara's greed that the Stone has become such a threat to the freedom of millions. In better hands, the Stone could have been put to such good use," he finished sadly.

"Marseahna, soon we are going to be leaving," Orion said quietly as he joined them. He put his arm around the young Verdanan. "Only L'Juntara is to blame," he said, fury blazing for a moment in his green eyes. "But one day, I promise, he will be at our mercy."

"But for now we must continue our preparations for a tactical retreat," Truestar interceded.

"Are we really going to fly?" Marseahna whispered excitedly. In her experience, ships belonged to gods, and were not trespassed upon by mere mortals. But that was in the past, Marseahna told herself, and these were people just like her. Soon she felt the strange vibration of the ship beneath her and heard the humming of the starship's engines as Stellara activated them.

As Orion and Marseahna secured themselves in the rear seats of the bridge, Stellara moved over to the co-pilot seat and Truestar took the helm. Expertly he guided the ship from its stone hangar deep within the core of the mountain. The *Eagalos* lifted easily from her landlocked sleep and glided toward the pinpoint of light at the far end of the tunnel. Then suddenly they burst into the open air, the *Eagalos* quickly picking up speed as Truestar sped at just below light speed away from Verdana.

Marseahna gazed with growing bewilderment as the only home she had known blurred into indistinct shapes and then the blue Verdana skies faded into the blackness of open space. Suddenly Marseahna found she was viewing Verdana as an object in the sky, much as she had viewed the three moons before. Orion, sensing her confusion, put a reassuring hand on hers as they awaited the certain encounter with L'Juntara's orbiting ship.

CHAPTER 16

"We've picked up a sudden surge of energy on the far side of the mountains just east of the village of Theos, L'Juntara," the helmsman of the flagship informed his supreme commander.

L'Juntara stopped his nervous pacing, his cape falling around him as he gazed at the helmsman questioningly.

"That was the village where the priests were overpowered and the girl found the crystal," the helmsman added nervously.

"Yes, I know that," L'Juntara said impatiently. "But why does Truestar leave his hole now?" he asked himself aloud, his voice showing a rare tone of puzzlement. "He is up to something, but he knows he can't hope to escape by outrunning my starship. He must have the Exoterra Stone with him and is using its power to try something. Break orbit at once." L'Juntara growled as his helmsman sounded the attack alarm throughout the warship. "Close in on that energy surge."

"It is their ship!" the helmsman said, altering the larger ship's course to intercept Truestar's craft.

"Pursue and capture," L'Juntara said, seeing the rapidly moving blip on his scanner that indicated the escaping *Eagalos*. "Communications Officer, open channels with the Confederation ship. Indicate that if they offer no resistance we will board them without damage to their vessel."

As the distance between the two ships closed, an evil smile of expectation formed on L'Juntara's lips. Taking the communicator himself, he addressed the rebels: "This is L'Juntara. Give up this foolish attempt to flee. Prepare to be boarded, or face destruction. Decide your own fates. You cannot outrun us, Truestar. Give up. You have lost. Your cause is finished and—"

"Commander!" the helmsman called out in surprised dismay. "Truestar's ship is lengthening the distance between us. They are out of range of our tractor beam and lasers. His speed is incredible. Soon he will be able to make the leap to hyperspace."

"Impossible!" L'Juntara said, his cheeks flushed with anger as he stared at the now-fading blip on the screen. "How can it be? Their engines are no match for ours. Fire a warning shot across their bow. Even if they are out of range, it will startle them and convince them that we are serious in our intentions," L'Juntara barked, ready to try anything to recover the Stone and Truestar.

The helmsman sucked in his breath in fear of his superior's reaction as he gazed at the now-empty scope. "They are more than out of range, L'Juntara. They are gone. They have made the transition to hyperspace."

"Gone!" he spat out the word as if it burned his mouth. "Truestar has escaped me?" he demanded incredulously, his face looking white and pinched as he faced the bitter realization that he had failed.

L'Juntara's strong hands tightened into impotent fists as he struck one down forcibly on the control panel. "Blast his soul into the galactic void," he swore, his body rigid with rage. "I'll have those fool priests sent to the mines of Lucar, where they can burn for their incompetence," he vowed.

"What course shall I set, L'Juntara?" Lieutenant Altos said as he replaced the helmsman who had been on duty. Barely able to contain his happiness at the news that his comrades had escaped, Lieutenant Altos repeated his question to L'Juntara, gazing at the sulking dictator with disguised joy that he had been outwitted.

"Back to Verdana. Recall all land troopers. Then back to Juntar." He paused uncertainly, for once unsure of himself, and not relishing a return to his home planet with his mission in ruins.

* * *

As the land troops were being recalled, L'Juntara began to pace up and down the small conference room behind the bridge, his silvery head thrown back as he pondered his next move. Only the Exoterra Stone could have increased Truestar's escape speed.

"What do you want?" L'Juntara bellowed angrily as his chief scientist interrupted his thoughts.

"My Supreme Commander, I have welcome news to bring you." The scientist smiled, knowing he would now be in his commander's good favor. "I, with the help of my staff, have activated the Exoterra crystal."

"What!" L'Juntara exclaimed with near disbelief, his gray eyes burning with increasing excitement.

"Yes, a combination of sound and light waves have activated the crystal. I took it upon myself to couple the crystal to the scanners and see if we could trace Truestar's vessel into hyperspace. We failed to trace him, but the increased power of the scanners registered a unique energy source on Verdana's surface."

"What kind of energy source?" L'Juntara asked impatiently.

"The readings are completely alien to anything we have seen before," the scientist continued in a state of excitement, "except that the source has the same composition as our crystal of Exoterra. It also is much larger—many times larger, L'Juntara."

"Then what you're saying is that you've located the *main* Exoterra Stone," L'Juntara said in a hoarse whisper. The scientist's spreading smile answered L'Juntara's question.

L'Juntara's eyes began to glow. He took a seat at the head of the table and heaved a sigh of relief, feeling once again in control of the situation.

"Shall I begin the recovery operation?" the scientist asked, jarring L'Juntara from his renewed dreams of glory.

"Yes, immediately," L'Juntara said, smiling his approval. Apparently, L'Juntara speculated, Truestar had hidden the main stone somewhere other than his own hiding place. When L'Juntara's troops searched the planet Truestar had been unable to get at the Exoterra Stone again. But Truestar must have had a piece of the stone that enabled him to boost his ship's engines and make his getaway. "Truestar must have hated to leave that stone behind on Verdana," L'Juntara said aloud to the two guards posted by the conference room door. He left the chamber for the bridge to view the recovery operation. His malevolent smile caused a twinge of fear to cross Lieutenant Altos's face when he turned to face the approaching commander.

"You think the Stone is actually on Verdana? I thought Truestar had escaped with it," Altos questioned innocently.

"He miscalculated," L'Juntara told him with relish. He then personally took control of the ship, proficiently guiding it close to the wild surface of the swamps of Verdana with a skill unequaled by even his best pilots. "Not that I wouldn't have done the same thing," he suddenly added with unusual candor. "But I wouldn't have run away without my treasure. That is where he made his biggest mistake. I would have stayed and fought to the death to keep control of that stone." He spoke with a vengeance that caused a chill to spread through Altos.

"You are directly over the power surge," the scanning scientist announced as he centered the large blip on his scope.

The recovery operation proceeded smoothly as the hovering starship's powerful tractor beam tore loose vines, trees, and slime from the swamp. At last the Exoterra Stone was lifted from the depths of the swamp, dripping and splattered with mud. But its brightness was not dulled, and it glowed steadily with a vivid turquoise color that caused several of the recovery crew to blink their eyes and then shield them from its piercing light.

"Recovery completed and successful, L'Juntara," the chief scientist announced. "Your *treasure* is secured on the hangar deck."

"Good," L'Juntara said simply, his thoughts already

on his next plan of action. "Communications officer, contact Juntar. Have all warships assemble at Station ACXII. There the Stone will be broken into crystals and each warship equipped with Exoterra power in its engines and lasers. No planetary defense shields can withstand that power. Yes, I believe it is time we met the enemy in its own camp. Set course for Doros after we pick up the fleet."

CHAPTER 17

The *Eagalos* sped through the star-blurred mist of hyperspace, carrying its precious cargo of four fugitive rebels. Orion glanced across at Marseahna, whose head was propped against the side of her seat. She dozed fitfully, the excitement of the past events almost too much for her.

"Marseahna's coping pretty well, all things considered," Orion said proudly as he gazed at the young Verdanan. "Too bad she had to get mixed up in all of this. Which Confederation planet are we heading toward?" he asked, leaving his seat to stand next to Truestar and Stellara.

"What was that, Orion?" Truestar asked, glancing up at the young Auranian. "I'm sorry; I was thinking of something else."

Orion shrugged. "Just idle curiosity on my part. When you find yourself speeding across hyperspace and see no familiar coordinates flashing on the navigation scope, you like to think that the pilot had some destination in mind."

"I understand your concern, my boy, and I compliment you on your knowledge of the star charts. Yes, this is uncharted space to all but a few merchants and scientists," Truestar said, readying himself for the prince's reaction.

"You mean we are heading *away* from the Confederation!" Orion exclaimed, both puzzlement and anger coloring his voice and abruptly awakening Marseahna from her slumber. "How come we're running away from our home planets when they may be under attack? The Juntariums murdered my family, and now millions more are threatened."

"And what could we do to help them?" Truestar replied resignedly, his sad tone soothing the prince's own feelings. "You know it as well as I do, Orion. My son, I can understand your anger. Stellara and I share it too. But until we find a way to destroy the Stone, we'll be of no help to anyone. And if we're captured, L'Juntara will scan our minds to learn the location of the main stone."

"Orion," Stellara said with tenderness, placing her arm around the blond prince. "Alex made a great sacrifice so that you would not fall into L'Juntara's hands. He hoped that we would reach Truestar, and we have. Alex knew that if L'Juntara ever discovered the extent of your Aura, he would destroy your mind to discover everything about this unique power."

"You're right, of course," Orion said after a moment of silence, a note of apology in his voice. "Doros and Aurania will be their prime targets. Do we have an actual destination? I assume you've been this way before," he added, a trifle worried.

Truestar laughed, a rare sound, coming from the scientist. "No, we aren't quite at the mercy of the unknown, Orion. I didn't leap blindly into hyperspace. Yes, I have come this way once before. It was a long time ago—almost in a different lifetime, it seems," he reminisced. "I discovered a wonderful planet. A very special one, in fact, and if the citizens of that planet will allow us to land, then I think, for a while at least, we will be safe and I will have time to figure out a way to destroy the Exoterra Stone."

"What's the name of this planet?" Orion asked, interested in learning of a human colony in this seemingly unpopulated sector.

"Ceanius." Truestar breathed the name with reverence, the word almost a caress.

"Ceanius?" Orion tried the word. "I've never heard of it before, and I thought I knew all the discovered worlds of the galaxy," the prince reflected, in confusion.

"Ah," Truestar said with a chuckle, "but you said 'discovered' worlds. This one remains undiscovered."

"You mean you never charted it or told anyone about it?" Orion asked in puzzlement. "Why not?"

"Because the Delphini, the inhabitants of Ceanius, asked me not to. And I agreed with their wisdom in wanting to keep their privacy. They only allowed my ship, the *Eagalos,* to land because we were in danger of burning up in their atmosphere. We'd suffered damage in a meteor shower and had to make repairs," Truestar explained. "And we could hardly repay their kindness in saving our lives by betraying their trust."

"But what of your crew?" Orion questioned curiously. "Might not one of them have spoken about the planet? Not everyone would be quite so selfless, I suspect," Orion remarked sagely.

"The only other crew members were Stellara and your uncle Alex," Truestar replied softly. "I would trust them with my life."

Orion nodded in understanding, the mention of Alex bringing a deep sadness to his eyes. "Yes, of course."

"So we took a vow never to speak of the Delphini or of Ceanius."

"Approaching Ceanius star system," Stellara called out as she switched the picture filling her visiscreen to a close-up of the planet ahead. The ship now dropped to sublight speed.

"Ceanius is the fourth planet out from its sun," Truestar told Orion as the planet began to grow larger on the small screen, eventually filling it entirely as they sped closer to the greenish-blue world surrounded by a wreath of wispy white clouds.

"Why, it's almost all water," Orion exclaimed. "I can only pick out a few land masses, and those are unbelievably small."

"Yes, the planet of the Delphini is over ninety percent water," Truestar informed Orion. With an indulgent smile, he innocently added, "Did I neglect to explain that the Delphini are a highly evolved form of water-inhabiting mammal? I suppose some less-knowl-

99

edgeable persons would consider them mere fish," Truestar added contemptuously, "but don't make that mistake. They are as intelligent as you or I, and with the exception of you, Orion, they are far superior to all others in extrasensory perception."

"Incredible!" Orion breathed in awe. "A planet populated solely by water creatures. Aren't there any humans at all?"

"No, but I believe there were at one time. The Delphini think that they were brought to Ceanius in great sky ships but, like ours, so much of their history is a mystery. But suffice it to say that now there are only the Delphini," Truestar explained to the young prince, glancing at him thoughtfully. "You know, I think you and the Delphini will get along famously. They are much like Auranians in their love of peace, and in the tranquility they have tried to maintain in their world. Yes," Truestar continued with a ruminative look in his eye, "I look forward to this meeting between you and the Delphini. It should prove to be quite an experiment. Yes, indeed."

The engines of the ship suddenly slowed as they entered the periphery of Ceanius's gravity field. The jolting of the ship reawakened Marseahna, whose eyes quickly focused on the vision on the screen and on the view from the side portals. She stared speechlessly at the planet revealed before her.

"Why should my meeting with them be so special?" Orion asked Truestar.

"Because of their highly developed psychic powers. Their power is so strong that their Aura shields have maintained a protective barrier around their planet in the upper atmosphere. The Delphini have somehow coupled their minds with the same mysterious gift of power that you possess, Orion. Now this barrier is self-sustaining, and guards them against any intruders. As you are aware, there are those in the galaxy unscrupulous enough to exploit even this gentle, magnificent form of life," Truestar said, obviously with L'Juntara in mind. "If others knew of their existence, it could

100

bring destruction to their way of life, even to their world."

"How will we get through the energy field?" Orion questioned. "The *Eagalos* isn't in danger of crashing this time. Do you think they will know we mean them no harm?"

"I was hoping that perhaps—" Truestar began, but stopped as he became aware of a strange look on Prince Orion's face. His green eyes seemed an extension of the green Ceanius seas now visible on the screen.

Marseahna observed her friend's sudden stillness and hurried to Orion's side. "Orion," she began, and reached out a tentative hand to the pale-faced boy. But Truestar's quick grasp of Marseahna's wrist stopped her from touching the prince.

"Leave him, Marseahna," he advised gently. "I believe he is under the influence of his Aura. He really isn't here with us." Truestar then glanced back at the screen still displaying the planet Ceanius.

Orion could almost feel the soft warmth of the sea as it surged around him, the gentle lapping of the frothy white waves lulling his mind with an almost hypnotic quality.

Out of the green depths a sleek gray form emerged, its smiling face and bright eyes gazing into his own. Orion opened his mind to probing, and felt no fear or strangeness as their minds merged and shared thoughts.

"It's all right, Truestar." Orion spoke suddenly, his voice warm with assurance. "The Delphini will let us land safely. They are concentrating now on creating a break in the barrier for us to pass through," he told them. Then he smiled in amusement as he told the momentarily startled Truestar, "They send a special welcome to you, Truestar, but ask why you've not honored them with a visit until now. They are grieved that it has been such a long time since they last saw the tall strangers who walk upon the land but have great wisdom for a human." Orion chuckled; then his smile faded as he addressed Stellara, who'd turned in her seat to hear Orion's happy words. "And they send greetings to the sad-eyed small one with hair like the sunlight. We are all bid welcome to Ceanius," Orion concluded, then slumped forward in his seat. But seconds later he pulled himself up, his face free of all the worry and sadness it had shown since his plunge to Verdana.

Orion glanced around the cabin curiously. "I feel so refreshed. I was in contact with the Delphini, wasn't I, Truestar? Oh, I can't even describe to you the experience. I've never felt quite such a sensation before. The peacefulness of it all seemed to wash over me, and I felt as if I'd known Xenos, the Delphini who spoke to me, for centuries."

Truestar was visibly affected by this incredible display of mental telepathy, even though he had hoped that Orion's power might enable him to contact the Delphini and inform them of their wishes to land. But he'd never imagined their communication would be quite so successful.

Recovering from his initial shock, Truestar rejoined Stellara at the controls as they started their descent to the planet's surface through the recently opened passage in the barrier. They followed a corridor through the barrier to an area of contrasting greens and browns that indicated a small island on Ceanius's surface. The *Eagalos* disappeared into a great cloud bank, a swirling mass of vapor that obscured their view of the planet below, until they broke out beneath and had an almost breathtaking view of emerald-green and turquoise-blue seas. The dot of brown that had been targeted as their landing site materialized just beneath them into a rocky island thick with dark green trees and sandy beaches. Stellara turned over the control of the *Eagalos* to Truestar, who with a steady and practiced hand guided the ship to rest on a rise of land overlooking a small half-moon bay.

"Engines off," Truestar said quietly, breathing a sigh of relief now that they had reached Ceanius safely. Truestar followed Stellara into the rear cabin, and with an encouraging smile to Marseahna and a wink at Orion, he pressed the release lever and the portal slid open.

Orion stepped out onto the sand and breathed deeply of the fresh flora-scented air. Now that the *Eagalos*'s engines had been shut down, the only sound was the whispering of the waves and the wind in the tall treetops above.

"It is just as beautiful as I remembered it," Stellara said more to herself than to anyone else, especially since Orion and Marseahna were already exploring the bay, drinking in the pure sunshine and brisk salty breeze.

"Look! What's that?" Marseahna called out in alarm as she saw strange gray shapes gliding through the waves toward the shore, where Orion was wading in the warm waters. "Orion! Get back on shore!" she cautioned, racing toward her friend.

Truestar laughed and caught Marseahna's arm as she passed by. "Come, let us properly greet our hosts, the Delphini," he advised as he and Stellara with Marseahna in tow walked toward the water's edge, where Orion was standing silently staring out to the breakwater.

"There must be hundreds of them coming in," Marseahna whispered as she stood slightly behind Truestar's flapping robes.

Every so often the gray shapes appeared, then dove deep beneath the surface of the azure sea. Some leapt into the air while others frolicked in small playful groups, but ever steadily they drew closer to the shore where the four people were watching them in bemusement.

Suddenly Orion startled the others when he broke free from the spell that had held them immobile on shore and waded hip deep into the sea. Soon he was surrounded by the gray bodies of the Delphini swimming around his lone figure. He smiled and nodded his head, and then without hesitation reached out and clasped one of the larger Delphini to his chest, his laughter carrying back to those on shore.

"This is Xenos, and they welcome us to Ceanius," Orion called back to his friends. A loud chorus of barking, whistling sounds accompanied his words as the Delphini splashed around Orion in the shallows, their large gray bodies gliding effortlessly beneath the aquamarine waters before surfacing to breathe again.

"How does Orion know all this?" Marseahna questioned in puzzlement, enjoying the antics of these strange creatures, some of whom were over eight feet long. She stared in amazement at their almost human-looking faces. One in particular reminded Marseahna of old Sanderan, the baker in Theos. Their eyes, she noted, seemed to hold so much expression.

"Orion has established a link of mental telepathy with the Delphini," Truestar explained. "He can read their thoughts and they can read his. When we were here before, we used our computer to record their speech, then the computer translated their high-pitched sounds into our language, and finally broadcast our replies back to the Delphini in their own language," Truestar concluded, then smiled broadly as he watched Orion in the water. "Of course, now the whole progress can be simplified, since we have a translator with us."

Stellara watched with an amused smile as Marseahna, with Orion's encouragement, rolled up her breeches and ran into the sea barefooted, her laughter joining the young prince's while they made friends with the water beings.

"For just an instant I would erase all of the years and wish to be young again like those two," Stellara said sadly. "If only one could forget all of the years in between," Stellara added with a shake of her blond head.

Truestar placed a comforting arm around Stellara's slight shoulders. "Some day I hope we may return here without any worries or cares and just soak up the gentleness of Ceanius," Truestar said with a sigh. "But not this time. Join me for a dip in the sea, so as not to offend our genial hosts, but after that we've got work to do."

"The Exoterra Stone?" Stellara guessed.

"Yes," Truestar said worriedly. "I did not like having to leave it on Verdana."

"But you had no choice—we were lucky to escape

with our lives," Stellara protested. "You've managed to save us all."

"But for how long, my dear?" Truestar asked. "It worries me greatly that L'Juntara has even one crystal of that stone. If I could learn its secrets, then eventually his top scientists will also. I must discover how to destroy the Stone before that calamity befalls us." Truestar added, impatience filling his voice, "I only wish I knew what was happening out there." He gave a longing look at the sky, which was now turning crimson as the sun of Ceanius began its fiery descent into the distant horizon line and the first stars began to dot the heaven. "I fear that time is running out for the Confederacy," Truestar said ominously, his fatalistic tone causing Stellara to turn from watching the two young people still frolicking with the Delphini. Their eyes met and held, filled with foreboding.

CHAPTER 18

The next day on Ceanius set a pattern for the following few days as Truestar and Stellara set up a makeshift laboratory and began a series of tests and experiments on their pieces of the Exoterra Stone. Since Orion and Marseahna could be of little help to them, they spent the lazy hours of each day swimming with the Delphini and exploring the rocky coves of the island.

But one afternoon while swimming, Orion had a sudden, terrifying vision, whose effect left him weeping long after the images had faded. Truestar and Stellara came running from the *Eagalos* laboratory to answer Marseahna's urgent summons, their faces mirroring concern. They found Marseahna wading ashore beside two Delphini, an unconscious Orion supported between the two gray creatures that ferried him into the shallows, where Marseahna was able to drag him onto the beach.

Truestar knelt down beside the pale boy, noting his rapidly beating heart. "What happened? Did he dive too deep?" he exclaimed.

"No," Marseahna answered, her voice shaking with fear. "He was laughing with me and Xenos and Rielos, when he suddenly gasped. Then his eyes rolled strangely, and he just seemed to sink beneath the water. Xenos started chattering excitedly, and then he and Rielos carried Orion safely to shore. Look," she said suddenly, pointing out to sea as a large gathering of Delphini swam closer, their unusual silence making Stellara and Truestar exchange uneasy glances.

"He's having a vision," said Truestar as he saw Orion's eyelids flickering. Then his eyes flashed open, their green irises glowing with a strange light that was almost turquoise in color.

"Doros!" Orion cried out in anguish. "Doros is falling! It is under attack. I can see a fleet of starships. I see a red planet and smaller ones, then shooting flames. They are Juntarium warships. They are attacking Doros; the planet's shields are failing. I see explosions on the planet's surface. Peres—Peres has been killed. The Confederate fleet is outnumbered but they continue to fight, but it's hopeless. The Juntarium ships are faster—so fast that they can't be destroyed. They seem to be armed with some superweapon that engulfs its target and then explodes it from within with unbelievable power," Orion gasped; then, in a spasm of pain, he screamed and writhed. "I see L'Juntara—he's laughing, an evil, cruel laugh as he gazes at the city below in flames. He's launching ground troops to take over the planet. Aurania will be next, and he intends to make it his capital. No!" Orion screamed in agony. The deathlike silence that followed seemed even worse than Orion's outburst. Orion's piercing voice echoed the cries of the thousands of dying people on Doros and the anguish of the nearly destroyed Confederate fleet that would not be able to defend Aurania, the next target.

Truestar got to his feet shakily from kneeling beside Orion, his face deathly pale as beads of cold perspiration broke out on his forehead. Stellara glanced up at him almost wildly.

"What are we to do? Can this be true?" she demanded.

Truestar's shoulders slumped perceptibly. "It is the end. It has come sooner than I thought." His eyes were dull as they turned to gaze out over the glistening ocean. "L'Juntara has found the Exoterra Stone. He has learned its secrets. Doros has fallen to him, Stellara. The Confederacy has suffered its greatest defeat, perhaps even its death blow."

Stellara scrambled to her feet, tears streaming down her face as she thought of her fellow Dorosians and the cruel deaths many of them must have suffered. "I can't believe it. Not Doros. Peres dead. It musn't have fallen. Orion is wrong. He can't have known what happened.

That's so many star systems away from here. Doros! Oh, Doros!" she cried desperately, knowing that Orion's words were true. She stumbled away from them across the sand.

Marseahna started to rise but Truestar's hand held her down. "Let her go; she needs time to cry. Doros was her home. Those people were her people that Orion heard cry out in fear and in pain. She must have time to heal her wounds. Time!" Truestar repeated in frustration. "It is time that is my worst enemy. If only I had enough time to discover how to destroy the Exoterra Stone."

Marseahna watched sadly as Truestar stood silently staring up into the darkening skies, a presentiment of what was to come, Marseahna thought with a newly acquired understanding of what was facing them. She remained silent, gently holding Orion's hard as she waited patiently for him to regain consciousness.

Marseahna gradually became aware of a strange sound floating eerily around her. At first she thought it was the wind in the trees, but the wailing noise was coming from the sea. And then the realization of what it was dawned on her. The Delphini were weeping. They had read Orion's mind and felt the deep anguish of his vision, and were now grieving with them for the loss of Doros and its people.

CHAPTER 19

The next few days the camp of the exiles was morosely silent. They all went about their usual activities mechanically, each of their thoughts occupied with what must be going on beyond the Ceanius star system.

Truestar was still conducting repeated experiments on the fragments of Exoterra Stone. But now his hands seemed to move with impatience and his eyes glowed with feverish anticipation when he stared down at the turquoise stones.

Orion had been observing him for the last few days, and was growing weary of these seemingly futile attempts to destroy the crystals. Nothing seemed to dull their brilliant, almost pulsating colors. Whether activated or not, the crystals seemed hopelessly indestructible.

Orion absently picked up one of the smooth crystals, rubbing it in his palm thoughtfully. "May I take this piece of Exoterra Stone to show Xenos?" Orion asked Truestar. "He wanted to know if he could see this stone that has caused so much change and trouble for all of us."

Truestar frowned, not wanting to lose sight of any piece of this cursed stone. But seeing the hopeful look in Orion's eyes, he shrugged. "All right, but please, do be careful. My own carelessness in losing the other piece has cost us all too dearly already." His attention was already back on his experiments before Orion had even left. The prince shook his head, saddened that Truestar was still assuming so much of the blame for all that had happened. Quietly he left the ship for the sea.

Reaching the water's edge, Orion swam out to meet

Xenos, who was floating aimlessly in the azure shallows of the bay.

"I will be careful with it, Orion. You needn't fear."

Orion grinned. "I trust you, Xenos. It's just that everyone who has come in contact with this piece of stone has suffered. I don't want this turquoise rock to hurt the Delphini. I wish we'd never come here."

"Then you would have never met me and never would have become my friend, Orion."

Orion heard the hurt in Xenos's thoughts as he spoke about their friendship. Then, with a sudden touch of mischief, the Delphini snatched the crystal from Orion's palm.

"Xenos!" Orion called out, but his friend had dived beneath the waves, the captured treasure held securely in his mouth.

"It is a beautiful stone. The color reflects the seas of Ceanius. It glows even beneath the depths and lights my way as I dive into this cave. All right. I'm coming back."

Orion breathed a sigh of relief when the gray shape reappeared above the surface and began swimming toward him. He glanced around as he heard the high-pitched squeals of several young Delphini playing nearby. They were involved in some kind of game, Orion thought, with an indulgent smile at carefree youthfulness, which he himself no longer felt capable of. He wondered why they were singing as they swam around in a circle and dove, only to reappear in a flying leap above the waves.

"It's just a silly rhyming song about a cycle of three hundred and sixty-five days. It is funny because Ceanius completes its orbit around its star in two hundred forty-three risings of its star. I do not know where that other number came from, but it is something we have always chanted as we try to catch each other. Just a game. Here is the stone, Orion. It is so warm, yet cold. It does not belong here on Ceanius, or anywhere in our galaxy. It will only bring destruction. Truestar is wise. It must be destroyed."

112

Orion thought briefly of the cave drawings on his home planet that spoke of a world with three hundred sixty-five days to one orbit around its star. Then his thoughts drifted back to the stone. He was especially amazed at Xenos's perception of the stone. Sensing Xenos's sudden nervousness, he quickly took the stone from the Delphini. How he hated this stone and all the pain it had brought. He glared at it, feeling his Aural field rising as he held the stone in his palm, itching to throw the crystal into the depths of the sea and be rid of it forever.

As he was staring moodily at the bright crystal, his thoughts centered on its hidden powers, his green eyes suddenly widened, for the piece of Exoterra started to grow hot against his skin, its shape seeming to alter. Orion's mouth opened in an instinctive cry of fear, but before he could fling the hated stone from him, it had disintegrated into dust before his very eyes.

For a stunned instant both Orion and Xenos stared at the flecks of harmless-looking gray dust clinging to Orion's palm, watching in amazement as the sea breeze lifted the particles and blew then into oblivion.

"W-what happened?" his voice squeaked, almost as highly pitched as the Delphini's.

"You destroyed the stone, Orion! How did you do it?" Xenos's excited thoughts struck at Orion's temples.

"Me?" Orion answered aloud, his expression incredulous. "But I did nothing, Xenos. I was just holding it in my palm, listening to those young Delphini playing, when the stone disintegrated," he explained as he went over the scene again in his mind.

"Oh, I will quiet them down," Xenos said, just as a particularly shrill squeal rent the air, causing Orion to wince.

"No!" Orion cried out suddenly, as an astonishing thought struck him. "It's sound, Xenos. That is what destroyed the stone. Sound waves!" Orion yelled, his excited voice attracting Marseahna, who'd been wandering along the shore.

"Anything wrong, Orion?" she called out in concern

113

as the young prince began to swim with deft long strides toward the shore. Xenos hurried after him, and soon Orion felt the sleek shape beside him. He threw an arm across Xenos's back and was quickly towed ashore.

"We've discovered how to destroy the Exoterra Stone, Marseahna!" Orion answered, running across the soft sand toward the ship beached higher up.

Marseahna fell in behind him, quickly catching up with Orion near the starship. Their abrupt entrance into the laboratory caused Stellara and Truestar to glance up in surprise.

"It's gone!" Orion cried out, his face expressing so many different emotions that the two were not certain what he was talking about.

"Gone?" You've lost the Exoterra crystal?" Truestar demanded, a flush of rare anger spreading over his gaunt cheeks.

"Gone! Yes, it is, but into oblivion, where it belongs," Orion continued excitedly. Then, as he seemed to become aware of their puzzled faces for the first time, he explained in exasperation, "Don't you understand? That piece of Exoterra Stone you gave me has been destroyed! It's dust, Truestar. Nothing more."

Truestar's mouth opened soundlessly before he found his voice, but it was Stellara who managed to speak first.

"You've destroyed the Exoterra crystal?" she whispered cautiously. "How?"

"Yes, how did you do it?" Truestar asked, his voice now calmer than Stellara's. His expression looked doubtful, now that he'd had time to recover from Orion's sudden news.

"It's sound waves, that's what destroyed it," Orion tried to explain.

"But we tried sound waves, Orion. They had no effect," Stellara interrupted.

"Not ordinary sound waves. Listen. Xenos and I were out in the sea and I had the stone in my palm, when it just started to disintegrate. It grew burning hot, then began to change shape and color, and suddenly it was

114

dust." Orion described what he'd seen, his description causing Truestar to narrow his eyes with interest.

"What kind of sound waves, then?" Truestar asked.

"Well, the young Delphini were singing nearby, and their shrill sounds hurt my ears. Their song was a strange combination of high-frequency notes. That is the only explanation I can think of," Orion finished.

Truestar turned excitedly to Stellara. "If it is the song of the Delphini, then this is the break we've been waiting for. Get a recorder, quick, and let's tape their song. There's only one way of proving Orion's claim, and that is by recreating the situation."

The young Delphini were more than willing to repeat their song, and soon the strange melody was recorded on computer tapes. While the shrill voices filled the air, the turquoise stone was held aloft in Truestar's palm and then began to grow hot and waver before the amazed audiences's eyes. And then miraculously it was no more.

Truestar laughed triumphantly. "We have found the key to the Exoterra Stone!" he exclaimed joyously. "Forgive me, I shouldn't take the credit." He chuckled as he glanced around at the smiling faces surrounding him. "Will you extend my most grateful thanks to the Delphini, for without them we would never have discovered this. Their song is such an unusual combination of notes. And thank you, Orion. I think you know what this discovery means," he added with quiet gravity.

"The Delphini are pleased that they could be of some service to the great scientist," Orion replied for his hosts.

"Now back to the laboratory for further tests," Truestar informed them. Orion caught a gleam of excited anticipation in his eye as Truestar contemplated the next steps in his experimentation.

Marseahna and Orion quickly followed Truestar and Stellara to the lab within the ship. "I feel a sort of odd connection to this turquoise stone," Marseahna explained, "since it was found on Verdana."

"I know what you mean," Orion agreed, moving

closer to the glass case in which another turquoise crystal had been encased for the experiment. "I feel a strange sense of possessiveness about it, too. Not that I'd want to keep it," he added hastily.

The tape of the Delphini's song was replayed, the voices causing the humans to make faces at the pitch of certain notes. They all gathered around the glass case, waiting expectantly for the stone to crumble as before. But they remained staring at the whole intact crystal in growing alarm as it remained unchanged.

"I don't understand," Truestar murmured thoughtfully as he continued to stare at the glowing stone. "Hmmmm. The sound waves have had no effect."

They all remained silent as Truestar stood slightly aloof, his eyes seeming to stare inward as he puzzled over the problem. "Light. It must be the conjunction of both light and sound that destroys the Exoterra Stone. And—" he paused meaningfully "—not just any sound."

"Orion was listening to the Delphini and the stone was exposed to the light of the sun," Stellara pointed out.

"Let's try something else, then," Truestar suggested. Under the artificial light inside the ship, turned as bright as the sunlight outside, and with the sounds of the Delphini bombarding it, all four humans held their breath and stared hypnotically at the stone. The turquoise glow began to brighten, then fade to a colorless gray as it exploded from within and turned to dust.

Marseahna grabbed Orion and impetuously kissed his cheek when the stone shattered. Orion returned her kiss with a hug. Truestar and Stellara's faces were wreathed in triumphant grins as wide as their young companions'.

"When bombarded by the unique combination of sound and light, the stone seems to emit a self-destruct signal that causes it to implode, crumbling into dust," Truestar postulated.

"Now we have what we need to defeat L'Juntara," Stellara announced. "All we have to do now is transmit that signal throughout his computer network and there-

116

by destroy the Stone that has given him his new source of power."

At the mention of L'Juntara, a heavy silence fell over the room, each one thinking what might happen in the days ahead. For although they now could destroy his Exoterra Stone, they still needed a plan of action.

"This calls for a celebration," Truestar said, not wanting to dampen spirits further. "Why don't you two get the Delphini to take you for a long swim? By the time you get back, we'll have something special prepared. I know you're getting tired of the reconstituted staples we had on the ship. Besides, the Delphini will want to know our latest news."

"They already have read my thoughts." Orion smiled. "But I'll tell them in person anyway." Taking Marseahna by the hand, he turned to leave the cabin, but then he stopped and cast a curious glance at both Stellara and Truestar. "I had a strange feeling of fear just now," Orion said worriedly, "but I can't make any sense of it. Maybe this day has had too much happen at once." He shrugged his shoulders. "Come on, Marseahna, let's take that swim. Xenos and Rielos are already at the beach." But his parting look at the two adults was curious.

CHAPTER 20

"Well, I hope you don't think you've fooled me," Stellara commented drily. "You barely fooled Orion. He suspected something."

"I purposely blocked my thoughts. Now that we have found the means to destroy the Exoterra Stone, we must leave Ceanius at once. The prince picked up something, but his Aura is too weakened right now to be of concern."

"I know you all too well, my dear." Stellara smiled, hugging the scientist tightly. "I knew all along that you would not take Orion or Marseahna along with us when we found out the way to destroy the Stone."

"You're correct, Stellara. As always." He sighed, holding her close to him. "But I want you to stay here with them. This might be a suicide mission, now that Juntarium forces control most of the Confederacy." But Truestar knew his words were falling on deaf ears.

"My placc is with you in the *Eagalos,* and if this is its last mission, then"—she drew a deep breath—"then more than ever I should be on board."

For a moment they held each other in the silence of Ceanius's twilight, broken only by the sounds of the Delphini far out at sea.

"If that's your wish, all right. We'll go, and the young ones will stay here." Truestar spoke somewhat sadly, knowing that Stellara would never change her mind. "We shall have to leave at once; too much time has passed already."

Stellara glanced out into the bright sunlight, her eyes drawn to the splashing and sounds of laughter from the surf, where Orion and Marseahna were swimming with a large group of the water beings. "I feel almost like a traitor, leaving them here. I've become so fond of them."

Truestar followed her gaze. "I know; I have as well. But at least they will have a better chance of surviving here on Ceanius, if we aren't successful," Truestar comforted her.

"We'll leave necessary provisions for them on the rocks near here," Truestar said. "Xenos must have read our thoughts about leaving, and yet he and Rielos are keeping them out at sea. The Delphini will help Orion understand why we have had to leave him and Marseahna here."

"What was that?" Marseahna asked curiously. "I thought I heard something."

Orion glanced around. The sun had set over an hour ago but twilight lingered, and a full moon was rising above the sea and the tall island trees, bathing the beaches in a pale silvery light. "I don't hear anything now. But it's time we head back to the ship. I know I'm ready for that celebration Stellara and Truestar promised. Seems strange, though, tha—" Orion stopped abruptly as he now heard a distant roar, recognizing it this time.

"The *Eagalos!*" he cried out in surprise. He grew more fearful when the engines accelerated. "Truestar and Stellara have started up the engines. Wait, I can feel something. Xenos, you and the other Delphini are clearing a path for them through the barrier. They're leaving without us."

Suddenly they saw a flash of light in the sky and then the silvery sheen of the *Eagalos* lifting gracefully over the island. As Orion stood paralyzed in the sea shallows, Marseahna joined him and put her arm around him, her eyes wide with confusion as she watched the ship gliding through the sky.

"They've left without us," Orion exclaimed. "I don't understand. I thought they were our friends; we trusted them."

"That is why they left you, because they do care

about your safety." Xenos's words intruded into Orion's thoughts. *"Truestar begs your forgiveness in deceiving you and Marseahna, but he had no choice. You are a prince, with a very special gift. He could not risk your life in this mission. And Marseahna is an innocent victim of this war. She should be back on her farm in Verdana. She and her people are not responsible for this time or this battle. It is not their fight."*

"You should have told me, warned me," Orion cried out as he climbed out of the water.

"B-but I didn't know," Marseahna answered in surprise; then, realizing he was talking to the Delphini, heard their squealing protest from the sea.

Orion turned away and began to walk back to their camp on the other side of the island. Their trip was one of silent misery as Marseahna joined him. They trod the familiar path up from the beach with heavy steps, each lost in thoughts of their abandonment.

Orion walked over to the now-empty landing site and stared down at the objects that had been left neatly stacked on the rocks by Truestar and Stellara. His initial flush of hurt and anger began to fade as he grew concerned for Truestar and Stellara, realizing the dangers of the flight ahead of them.

"Hey, Orion," Marseahna called as she rummaged through the pile. "Here's a recorder. Do you think they left us a message?"

Orion pressed the tab, his eyes meeting Marseahna's as the familiar cellolike tones of the Confederate scientist boomed into the still night.

"Orion, Marseahna, I hope you will forgive us. I suspect that right now you are feeling only betrayal and anger. I suppose, had I been in your position, I would feel the same way. But these are difficult times, and we must try to set aside our personal feelings. There was no point in your accompanying Stellara and me on this mission, a mission that might end in destruction for more than just the passengers of the *Eagalos*. We will attempt to destroy all fragments of the Exoterra Stone with the new information we have discovered. To do this, however, we must go to the source of the power, and that means traveling into Juntarium space, perhaps even to Juntar itself, but we've no other choice, if we are to save the remnants of the Confederacy.

"We have left you provisions for several months and of course there is a natural food supply on the island and in the sea, which should support you. The caves you found during your exploration of the island can serve as your shelter. Orion, I have left something for you. It is wrapped up in that small box by the recorder."

Orion glanced down at the box, reaching out and opening it as Truestar's voice continued.

"It is a medallion that I have worn for many years. Your uncle, Alex, had three of them made. One for himself, one for Stellara, and one for me. It is a sculpture of the Delphini. We three once shared a happy time here on Ceanius, and now I want you to have the medallion as a keepsake. Because it was made by Alex's own hands, it will have special meaning for you."

There was a pause on the tape as Orion gazed in fascination at the delicately wrought medallion that hung from a heavy golden chain. A Delphini was depicted in all its natural beauty and grace in the golden metal, its laughing face pointing upward above the waves. Orion swallowed painfully at this reminder of Alex.

"I have taken the precaution, Orion, in case Stellara and I fail on our mission," Truestar's voice continued, "of securing a microscopic recording dot containing the Delphini song, behind the Delphini's eye in the medallion. Someday you may have need of it, but I pray that is not the case. Stellara and I now bid you both farewell, Orion and Marseahna. You have become like our own son and daughter. Until we meet again. Farewell."

Marseahna stood, silently staring down at her bare feet, her expression giving little away until she sniffed back her tears. Carefully Orion placed the medallion about his neck, his fingers holding it close to his chest.

"Well, I don't know how we're going to be of any help

122

to anyone, stranded here on Ceanius," Orion said gruffly, trying to disguise the heaviness of his heart.

"You don't blame me anymore, Orion?" Xenos inquired hesitantly, his thoughts coming to Orion from out at sea. *"I'm sorry I didn't warn you, but Truestar said nothing until they were about to leave, and his thoughts begged me not to tell you. I could understand his wisdom. It was not my place to interfere. You have shielded your mind from me, Orion. I grieve for the loss of your friendship."* Xenos's last words were tinged with sadness as his thoughts faded on the breeze.

"No! Don't go!" Orion cried out. "Xenos! Please forgive me my momentary anger. I deeply desire your friendship," Orion called out as he ran down to the water's edge, wading out until it slapped around his knees. "I know there was nothing you could have done. Even if you had warned us, there was no way we could have persuaded Truestar to take us with them. You saved us a bitter farewell, Xenos."

There was silence for a minute, then Orion breathed a sigh of relief as he saw the familiar gray shape gliding through the water, followed by other less quiet Delphini, who began calling out greetings from the breakwater as they approached the solitary figure standing in the shallows.

"And don't you leave me either," Orion whispered softly, sensing that Marseahna had joined him in the tidal pool. "I have come to value your friendship enormously," he concluded, putting his arm around her slender waist, feeling the softness of her long dark hair brush against his shoulder.

Marseahna gazed into Orion's green eyes, his hair nearly silver in the moonglow. "As I do yours, Orion." She spoke softly as she gently kissed his cheek.

They remained in the shallows, with the Delphini gliding next to them, until the first hint of dawnglow appeared in the horizon.

"I wonder where they are now," Marseahna asked curiously, also wondering which of the stars fading in the sunrise was the sun of her own Verdana.

Orion, reading her thought, pointed it out to her, barely visible in the now-brightening sky. Then they bid farewell to the Delphini and stretched out on the warm sand, where they fell exhausted into slumber that lasted until the sun of Ceanius was midway through its daily circle of the heavens.

CHAPTER 21

On board the *Eagalos,* Truestar and Stellara maintained an uneasy silence, both experiencing a twinge of conscience, although certain they had done the right thing as far as Orion and Marseahna were concerned.

"What is our estimated time of arrival on Hacohana?" Truestar asked as he watched the mist of hyperspace flashing by at even a greater speed than usual.

"Within the hour," Stellara replied, computing the course for the transition to sublight speed when they reached the fourth planet of the Macohana system, the nearest Confederation base to Ceanius. "Do you think that Macohana IV will still be in our hands? Or maybe it's destroyed, or—"

Truestar shook his head. "I'm not certain about anything anymore, but it is a calculated risk we must take. We can't hope to destroy the Exoterra Stone by ourselves. Even with our knowledge of the Stone, we must have help. If we find other Confederation ships on Macohana, we can outfit them with our remaining crystals. Then we all can travel at top speed and try to slip behind Juntarium lines. We must capture a Juntarium warship intact, or a base. Any computer link in the Juntarium network will do. If we destruct one crystal of Exoterra and transmit that signal throughout the central network, every ship and facility equipped with Exoterra boosters will suffer a sudden power loss as the crystal boosting it self-destructs. A warship traveling at high speed boosted by Exoterra rays could be torn apart by the sudden loss of power and uncontrolled change of speed," Truestar explained to an intently listening Stellara, who up until this time had wondered about and doubted the possibility of the success of their mission.

Stellara remained silent for a second, then looked at Truestar with a troubled gaze. "You do realize," she said carefully, "that once we destroy our pieces of Exoterra Stone, and if we succeed in our mission, then we will find ourselves behind enemy lines."

Truestar held out his hand and Stellara placed hers trustingly in it. "I know, my dear," he said gently, "and that is why I would have preferred to have you stay back on Ceanius with Orion and Marseahna."

"And I would not have missed this opportunity of destroying L'Juntara's threat for anything, or," Stellara added with a soft look on her face, "being here with you."

They stared into each other's eyes for a moment in recognition of their deep feelings for each other, and felt a tragic sadness that their life together might be ended shortly. But there was little time for their personal concerns.

Turning back to her scanner, Stellara noted the Macohana star system, its outer planets mere flashes on the viewing screen. "Stand by to drop to sublight between orbits of fourth and fifth planets," she ordered.

The whine of the engines changed as first the Exoterra booster was disconnected, then the standard hyperdrive. The *Eagalos* dropped below light speed, and the galaxy came into clear focus again.

At just below light speed they neared the fourth planet, passing quickly by its most distant moon, when suddenly a row of blips blinked on Stellara's scanning scope. "It's a squadron of ships," she said, trying to keep her voice steady.

"Whose?" Truestar asked quickly, afraid of the answer.

"They're not ours. Too large," Stellara said grimly as she scanned them. "Juntarium warships!"

"Confederation vessel. Macohana IV is now a part of the Juntarium empire. Tie in your ship's computer to ours at once and follow these coordinates to our ground base. If you fail to follow these instructions, you will be immediately destroyed by order of L'Juntara," a mechanical human order was voiced from the lead ship of the fleet that now surrounded them.

"This is our chance, Stellara, even though we are bound to be destroyed in the explosion as well. If we insert this Delphini recording into our computer and shine the light of this flare," Truestar said rapidly, bending down to grab a space flare, "with the Exoterra crystal already inserted into our computer, we can activate the self-destruct signal."

"And since our computer is linked with the Juntarium network, that signal would be transmitted throughout—"

"Here goes," Truestar said firmly as he activated both the flare and the Delphini recording. "I love you, Stellara," he said, gently kissing her lips for what he felt would be the last time.

But the crystal in the computer of the *Eagalos* remained as intact as before, as well as the *Eagalos* and the Juntarium fleet.

There was a prolonged silence gripping them as they waited for what seemed endless seconds, then suddenly an imperious voice again sounded from the lead warship. "Cease those high-pitched transmissions at once. There're no Confederates left to rescue you. Cease those coded messages."

"It didn't work! We have failed." Truestar spoke in a voice so full of pained disbelief that Stellara felt herself choking back a sob.

"I don't understand. We experimented on this procedure. We destroyed the crystals time and time again, before our own eyes," Stellara said as she tried to convince herself that this could not be happening. "We have repeated the same steps exactly. We've duplicated the formula. There can be no mistake."

Truestar stared down at his hands, and frowned with deep concentration. "No," he said so softly that Stellara had to strain to hear, "we have miscalculated. We have *not* reproduced the conditions of the experiment exactly," he said in a rising tone of voice, his face showing self-contempt. "I have been such a fool!"

"I don't understand. What did we fail to do? We

had the identical sound and light that Orion did when he first discovered the key to destroying the Exoterra Stone. We destroyed crystals ourselves three times."

"Yes, but we didn't have Orion this time," Truestar said flatly, his eyes looking meaningfully into Stellara's. "It is not only light and sound, but a combination of both of those *with* the Aura powers of our young friend that destroys the Exoterra Stone, causing it to emit its signal for its own self-destruction."

Stellara looked at the visiscreen showing the Juntarium ships surrounding them and knew that there would not be any escape for them this time. "The Aura," she said softly, tears falling from her violet eyes. "And we left him stranded on Ceanius."

"Prepare to be boarded!" a coldly triumphant voice commanded. "We have discovered your ship is the *Eagalos,* ship of the fugitive scientist, Truestar. This is your last warning. Do not resist. Instead of landing on Macohana, prepare yourselves for our tractor beam. On direct orders from L'Juntara, you are to be transported immediately to Juntar. Do not resist or we have orders to destroy your ship."

Truestar's hand automatically went to the button that Stellara knew would self-destruct the *Eagalos* immediately. Through reddened eyes she gazed at the scientist and nodded her approval of his decision.

Suddenly Truestar withdrew his hand from the switch.

"Why?" Stellara asked numbly, having prepared herself for death rather than L'Juntara's mind-destroying probes.

"Because I refuse to give up hope yet," he answered softly. "We will reach our destination after all, although not quite in the manner we had planned. At least we will be on Juntar, where the main computer system is located. As I suspected, L'Juntara has probably fragmented the Stone into countless parts to equip his warships and weaponry and to augment the power of his computer outlets. We might have another chance to destroy it."

"How?" Stellara demanded, less sure of their chances

than Truestar apparently was. "We still don't have Orion and his Aural power at our disposal."

"Orion." Truestar repeated the name, his thoughts centered on the young Auranian prince. "Orion, Orion, Orion." He said the name over and over again, sending his thoughts out through space and back to Ceanius. He pictured the greenish-blue planet as he'd last seen it. He filled his mind with aquamarine seas stretching into the horizon line, and the small rocky island they had landed on. He thought of the Delphini, sending his thoughts to them swimming in the blue depths. Finally, on a surge of energetic thought, he brought Orion's image into his mind's eye. He stared inwardly into the green eyes of the mystic prince, every cell in his body concentrating on the image.

"Truestar?" Stellara spoke in growing concern as she stared at the pale countenance of the great scientist, his eyelids flickering as cold sweat beaded his brow. His whole body seemed to be quivering and shaking with some kind of inner excitement or stress. Stellara became aware of the scraping sounds outside the hull of their ship and realized the *Eagalos* had been towed aboard the lead warship, and that soldiers would soon break through the portal into the rear cabin of the *Eagalos*.

Truestar slumped forward, his breathing shallow. "He will come, Stellara." And then he lost consciousness and fell across the console.

CHAPTER 22

Orion stared up into the blackness of the night sky, where a myriad of stars seemed to be beckoning, almost mocking him, he thought unhappily. Beside him Marseahna was letting her fingers slide through the warm sand, the coarse grains rubbing abrasively against her smooth skin. It was the second night since Truestar and Stellara had embarked on their mission. Orion and Marseahna sat holding each other close, beside a campfire they had built with some driftwood on the beach near the tideline.

"Aurania must not have been attacked yet," Orion said curiously. "I know I would have felt it since I felt the attack on Doros. My Aura senses are so heightened here; they've never felt stronger. They blend with those of the Delphini. Aurania must be mourning for Alex, and for me as well," the prince reflected, recollecting his last glimpse of his uncle as he and Stellara plunged toward Verdana aboard the space capsule.

"I've always felt restless," Marseahna said, absorbed in her own thoughts as she stared hard at the stars, "and wished to see beyond the mountains of Tor Cloudtopt, never believing that someday I would see beyond the stars."

Orion pulled Marseahna closer to him. "You'll never be the same, now that you've traveled to the stars, Marseahna. You know the future. You've traveled beyond the point where your planet would have been thousands of cycles from now. Now that Verdana is in the hands of L'Juntara, they will be propelled into the future. They will go through such a culture shock," Orion added almost sadly, "they'll lose their innocence."

"I wonder if we will ever see our home planets again,"

Marseahna asked; then, gazing out to the shallows where Xenos and Rielos were frolicking, she smiled. "But I doubt that Truestar could have picked a better place to leave us stranded," she added quickly.

Orion shrugged. "Ceanius, even though shielded by the Delphini from prying eyes and scanners, lies on one of the trading routes very seldom used. I remember that Truestar mentioned that though ships passed, the planet remained uncharted because the Aural shield, the same that I am gifted with, blocks any lifeform readings."

"We've had to increase our force shield this last cycle because trespassers have passed more and more frequently since L'Juntara has expanded his empire," Xenos confided as he swam nearby in the shallows. *"They are always curious when they pass close to Ceanius, and try to establish an orbit around us, but soon they discover that Ceanius has a strange gravitational force field which screens the planet and prevents exploration as well as scanning. They become discouraged after a while, and leave orbit. We are considered an inhospitable planet, I believe."* Xenos chuckled, and several other Delphini swimming nearby shared his humor.

"What are they laughing about?" Marseahna wanted to know.

"Oh," Orion responded casually, "just a little joke Xenos made."

"I wish I cou—" Marseahna began, when suddenly she became aware of her friend's shaking body. Then Orion gasped and grabbed his head, holding it as if trying to keep it from exploding from within.

"Oh, no," Orion moaned. "No, no, don't want to see this, please, no," he cried out as he curled himself up and tried to fight off the visions.

Marseahna knelt beside Orion, unable to do anything for the prince as she watched in silent helplessness while Orion writhed on the sand. His face was soon streaming with tears.

"They've been captured." Orion's rasping voice startled Marseahna. "They've been boarded by a Juntarium warship. I can see it all so clearly. They are going to be taken to Juntar. Stellara and Truestar sitting in the *Eagalos* while the ships surrounded them. A tractor beam has pulled them inside one of the ships. One of the guards has slapped Stellara across the face for something she said. They've pushed Truestar into a dark detention cell. He looks so old, so beaten all of a sudden. Oh, Marseahna, I can't stand to see them like this," Orion said thickly as he hid his face in his hands. "Truestar called out to me. He reached my Aura perception. He's saying we must come to them. But how?"

"W-what happened?" Marseahna asked in confusion, wiping Orion's matted hair away from his sweaty brow and holding him close to her.

Orion shook his head. "It didn't work. They had the correct light and sound and were even tied into the Juntarium computer network, but one thing was missing. It was *my* Aura power with the light and sound waves that caused the Exoterra to implode. Every time we experimented on a crystal, I was gazing at it, my senses heightened and my Aura field reaching out, combining with the light and sound waves."

"By the twin moons of Verdana," Marseahna sighed, sucking in her breath. "Was there ever such a stroke of bad luck?"

Orion rubbed his eyes dry. "I could feel Truestar's thoughts inside my head. It was as if he were sitting right where you are now and talking to me," Orion explained. "He willed me to see it, to hear him."

Marseahna spoke hesitatingly. "Well, I don't understand it all, but I do believe you, Orion."

"You saw it all too, didn't you, Xenos?" Orion asked.

"Yes, we all felt the agony of their capture and the thoughts Truestar was trying to send to you. He is right, Orion. You must go to Juntar if you are to stop this madness. Even though we hate to see you leave," Xenos added sadly and his feelings were echoed by sad squeals in the distant seas.

"We can help you, Orion," Xenos said suddenly, his squealing now changing to a calmer tone. *"There is a merchant ship passing through this system soon. When*

133

*it reaches our gravitational pull, our combined Auras
can cause its engines to fail. It can be brought down and
you can use it as your transport."*

Orion ran into the shallows and joined the Delphini.
Suddenly he felt his Aura blending with theirs, and he
could see the battered merchant vessel in the upper
reaches of Ceanius's atmosphere. The prince could
make out the faces of the confused old captain and his
crew as the ship's engines failed. Suddenly the ship was
pulled down through the thick cloud banks of a strange
planet that they had not even been able to scan seconds
before.

"It's working, Xenos!" Orion cried, his voice seeming
to blend with the squeals of the Delphini.

*"I knew it would, Orion. For the bond between us
and the Auranian prince is eternal, and that is what
gives us strength,"* Xenos said, swimming next to Orion
in the shallows.

On the shore Marseahna's eyes widened as she saw
the shape of a starship appear through the tangle of
white clouds above the island's surface, its battered hull
tinted amber by the first rays of dawn.

CHAPTER 23

Orion and Marseahna raced excitedly toward the downed spacecraft that had landed on the former site of the *Eagalos*. Orion was still a little pale from exerting his Aura power to assist in its landing, but he was able to keep up with Marseahna's easy strides. Considering the age of the ship it seemed to be in fairly good shape, Orion thought, noticing the wear and tear on the vessel from years of trading in odd parts of the galaxy. But Marseahna was less kind in her assessment of it.

"It sure doesn't look like much, Orion," she said in disappointment, having seen only the shiny ships of L'Juntara's fleet and Truestar's special *Eagalos*. To her inexperienced eye, this ship looked bulky and dingy, its dull metal hull showing dents and repairs.

"It's a merchant trading ship, Marseahna," Orion informed her as they waited anxiously for some sign of life from within. "They aren't built for speed or beauty. They're like—" he paused, trying to think of a comparison Marseahna would understand, "—they're like your finest festival tunic compared to your plain woolen work tunic. Both serve their own purpose."

Marseahna nodded, but she still felt spacecraft should be shiny and sleek. "I wonder who is inside."

"Yes, I wonder," Orion thought uneasily. Traders were a notorious group of wanderers, some of whom bordered on piracy, and few felt allegiance to anyone but themselves. They seldom frequented the ports of Aurania. And in fact, they were usually politely but firmly discouraged from such trade. Aurania's peaceful cities and cultural pursuits offered little diversion for the bolder and rowdier star traders.

The portal of the *Star Dancer* slid open and a bizarre

figure in a belted, loose-sleeved, knee-length robe of bright reds and blues stepped out. He had a long, curly beard of black streaked with gray, and curly locks partly hidden beneath a purple and yellow scarf wrapped in intricate folds around his head and neck.

Marseahna's dark eyes opened wide as she took in this colorful figure, her eyes lingering on the boots that nearly touched his knees and were trimmed in some kind of exotic fur.

"A Mercai," Orion muttered more to himself than to Marseahna, who was still openly staring at the ship's captain.

"A what?" she whispered, moving closer to Orion.

"A Mercai," Orion repeated with a sigh. "They're the most infamous of all merchant traders. They claim they can outfight and outdrink anyone in the galaxy, and wherever they travel, they try to prove it. If there's trouble, than they're usually in the middle of it."

"How do you know he's one?" Marseahna whispered, noticing for the first time the man's yellow-tinted eyes.

"By the style of dress, the beard, and," Orion added as he met the Mercai's steady gaze, "the eyes."

"By the long days of Botavar!" the Mercai exclaimed as he walked across the sands to where Orion and Marseahna were standing. "Am I star-crazed or hallucinating that I see two young humans before me on what I thought must surely be an uninhabited planet?"

"No, we are quite real," Orion replied calmly. "I am Noiro of Ro-Kien, and this is my friend Marseahna. We sure are glad to see you. You see, we've been stranded here since our starship had engine trouble and crashed on this planet," Orion fabricated, deciding to keep his true identity a secret. "Only, we didn't have as lucky a landing as you. We landed in the sea, and our ship sank. We are the only two survivors."

"Ro-Kienish, eh?" the Mercai said, glancing intently at the two young people. "I am Camrey, of T'Shan. You're a long way from your home, Noiro of Ro-Kien. What brings you so far adrift?"

"War, Camrey of T'Shan," Orion responded eagerly.

136

"My girl friend and I have left Ro-Kien. We want to join in the adventure and seek glory. There is little work on Ro-Kien since the merchant guilds have seized control."

Camrey rubbed his beard thoughtfully. "And what was your destination?" he asked softly as he watched them carefully.

"Juntar, of course," Orion replied, as if surprised by the question, his answer catching Marseahna off guard.

"Ah, no Confederation sympathies here, eh?" he chuckled.

"We of Ro-Kien always prefer to be on the winning side," Orion responded easily, his grin sly. "But why should you wonder? I've been told that the Mercai have no allegiance to any but themselves, and acknowledge no master."

"You've heard right, then, Noiro," Camrey responded with a fierce look, which was quickly replaced by a friendly grin. "But if you're thinking of catching a ride with us, you'll have to think once again, because it would seem as if the *Star Dancer* is planet-bound. Besides, we weren't heading to that bleak world L'Juntara calls home."

"Perhaps your ship wasn't damaged too severely. You certainly seemed able to handle her well when you landed," Orion complimented Camrey.

"Well," Camrey said hesitantly, "I'm not really sure what went wrong, just that I lost control and directional steering until we'd passed through the atmosphere."

"That's just what happened to us," Orion lied. "It must be this planet's unique gravity that affects our controls—some mineral, perhaps?"

"Yes, I suppose so," Camrey agreed. "It wouldn't hurt to check the controls out. But I don't fancy staying here for long, even though it is beautiful. Any life at all?"

Orion shrugged. "Fish, that's about all. No intelligent life forms at all."

"Thanks, I'll remember that the next time you want

137

a free lift out beyond the waves," Xenos's voice complained with mock anger.

"Well, I'll get my crew to check out the *Star Dancer*," Camrey said, glancing at his ship nestled in the sand. "I don't think there has been any structural damage, but it won't hurt to make sure, after I've got the controls working."

It wasn't long before Camrey returned with the news that the ship was fully operational, his features showing both relief and confusion. "I don't understand it. I'd sure have thought that at least one wire was loose, but by the Gases of Wiss, that ship is entirely operational. We can take off at any time."

Orion said quickly, "That's terrific. I trust that we might come to some mutually advantageous arrangement for transport on your vessel."

Camrey trained his trader's sharp eye on the pale-haired young man. "Well, I won't leave you and the young lady stranded here, but I'll only take you as far as I'm bound, and that's the stars of my home, T'Shan. Unless of course," he added craftily, "you make me an offer well worth my while."

Orion frowned. T'Shan was almost in the opposite direction from Juntar. What, he wondered, could possibly be worth trading for a trip to Juntar? All they had in their possession were the provisions left by Truestar and Stellara, hardly enough to cause a Mercai captain to change his route to Juntar.

"We will hate to see you and Marseahna leave Ceanius, Orion. But we know that you must leave to help your friends and save your home worlds. There are many treasures beneath the sea, which few ever discover. We will provide your fare to Juntar, Orion. Just have the captain bring some of his crew with you to the far side of the island in an hour, no sooner. In the small cove you will find something worth trading. I have read the captain's mind and I know what is of value to him. Something the Mercai will covet."

A slight smile parted Orion's lips as he thanked Xenos silently and said offhandedly to Camrey, "Of

138

course, we do have something which might be worth trading for our passage to Juntar." Orion continued calmly, ignoring Marseahna's incredulous glance. "It's on the far side of the island, in a cove. We can eat something here, and then we'll have to wait an hour before the tide recedes in order to gain entrance to the cove."

Not knowing what to expect, Orion led them an hour later to the cove. He was as surprised as the merchant by the stunning sight that left them speechless for several seconds, overcome by the beauty of the scene.

Piled high on the sand, where the waves lapped against the rocky shore, was an amazing assortment of shells that took their breath away. Pink-tinged coiled shells and spiny-ribbed brilliant red ones vied for attention with smoothly rounded shells gleaming in a rainbow of colors. But what held the eye were the giant shells. Larger than a man, some of them were, standing eight feet high, their curving interiors a shining wall of pearl.

"By the magic of the Elders of Casioc, this is indeed a treasure, my boy, yes, indeed," Camrey breathed, the awe of this discovery glowing in his eyes. "How did you find these?"

"There was a storm and they washed up onto shore. We came upon them one day while hiking through the woods," Orion improvised silently grateful to Xenos and the other Delphini.

"You don't need to thank us, Orion. We wish we could do even more to help you on your quest. But I know we will meet again, in a brighter time."

"Farewell," Orion said, his eyes brimming with the knowledge that he might never see Ceanius again.

"Farewell?" Camrey asked, overhearing the blond young man.

"Yes, I was just bidding farewell to this beautiful place," Orion said, lifting one of the shells. "Do you think these might cover our fares to Juntar, Camrey?" he asked jokingly.

CHAPTER 24

As the *Star Dancer* approached Juntar, it became clear that the planet had none of the natural beauty of either Verdana or Ceanius. It was a rusty-colored planet, devoid of the blues and greens that would indicate forests and seas. Orion knew some of Juntar's turbulent history. During their civilization's race for advancement, Juntar had fallen victim to wars and the problems of runaway technology, a combination that had destroyed the delicate balance of nature. The air had become too poisonous to breathe, and the people were forced to build domed cities in order to filter the air flow and make it suitable to breathe. Outside the domed cities, life on the planet's once-fertile hills, valleys, lakes, and forests became extinct. High winds swept across the land that was now vast deserts.

While aboard the *Star Dancer,* Orion and Marseahna had learned that most of the Confederacy had fallen, and that many of the outlying worlds had erupted into civil warfare. The hub of the Confederation, Doros, was now under occupation by Juntarium forces. Aurania itself was in a state of blockade, and only an inexplicable malfunction in L'Juntara's flagship had saved Orion's world from occupation or total destruction. When L'Juntara's hyperdrive had failed, he had turned back, not wanting the occupation of this prized conquest to be led by anyone else. Camrey had told the visibly shaken prince that the rumor was that L'Juntara intended to make Aurania his new capital, seeking to inhabit a world where domed cities were unnecessary. This much-dreaded prospect made the quest to destroy the Exoterra Stone even more important to the young prince.

After disembarking from the *Star Dancer,* Camrey

and his crew had loaded their precious cargo aboard the ground transit and set course for the Tombs, the oldest quarter of the city, where traders from all sectors of the galactic region came to barter their wares.

"Camrey!" a short balding man with a wide, toothy grin called out from the doorway of one of the many storefronts on the narrow crowded merchant street. He held out his arms to engulf the *Star Dancer*'s captain in a bearlike hug. "You never fail to surprise me. I'm nearly speechless, seeing you here on Juntar."

"Ah, but who but Sa-Baran would I come to if I wanted to trade the most unique goods this side of the 'Void of Forever'?" Camrey said, eager to unveil his new-found treasures.

"Well, what have we got this time, Camrey?" Sa-Baran asked, feigning only mild interest. "No more scents from the Karsoming system. The market's flooded with them. I warn you, I can't pay the top price."

"No, not that, but something very special. Something I'll wager you've not seen in many a season," Camrey said enticingly, pulling forward one of the crates. Removing the lid with a grand gesture, he pulled out one of the shells the Delphini had given them. Sa-Baran's usual businesslike demeanor crumbled with surprise and pleasure as he carefully held the shell in his hands, forgetting to maintain his normal disinterested trader's façade.

Camrey glanced over at Orion and Marseahna and winked, knowing he would be able to ask any price he wanted from Sa-Baran and get it.

"Now, my young friends, I'd suggest," Camrey began, when he was interrupted by a strange gasp from Orion. Marseahna realized what was happening to her friend before Camrey could respond. She moved quickly to Orion's side, her arm supporting his crumbling figure.

"What's wrong with Noiro?" Camrey asked in puzzled concern as he rushed to give Marseahna a hand. His strong arms neatly scooped the slumped form of Orion and laid him down gently on the floor by several

142

large woven baskets filled with the exotic scents of spices.

"What's happening to him?" Camrey asked once again as he eyed Orion worriedly, noting the paleness of his face and the throbbing vein standing out in his throat. "Is he ill?"

"No, he's just having a vision," Marseahna replied calmly, now accustomed to her friend's strange attacks.

"A v-vision?" Camrey repeated in an uncharacteristic, timid tone of voice. The Mercai were an extremely superstitious race of people. They still believed in curses and spells and magic potions and in the mystic powers of certain "chosen" people. Camrey now quickly stepped backward from the prone form of the pale-haired lad, of whom he'd grown fond. He made a strange sign, his fingers closing tightly around the odd assortment of medallions and charms he wore on several chains around his neck. But Orion's next startlingly clear words caused the Mercai captain even greater fear.

"Someone on your crew has turned us in, Camrey. Someone found my image on your computer file and broadcast a message to L'Juntara. His troopers are looking for us now."

Camrey was mesmerized by the glowing emerald eyes of Orion, eyes that seemed to be staring right through him and into his soul. He gave a great shiver of relief when soon their intensity and vibrant green color dulled.

Marseahna helped Orion to his feet. For a second he leaned on her shoulders, then took a hesitant step forward. His expression was surprised when Camrey moved with uncommon speed from his path.

"Camrey?" Orion questioned in puzzlement.

"You had a vision, Orion," Marseahna told him quietly.

The shadows lifted from Orion's eyes and he nodded slightly. "Yes, I'm beginning to remember now," he said with an apologetic look at Camrey.

"Who are you?" Camrey found his tongue at last, feeling oddly ill at ease now with this strange boy.

"That's not important, but our presence here with you can only get you into trouble, Camrey," Orion told him gravely. "We must leave. Thank you for your help, Camrey. I'm sorry I can't explain more," Orion told him sincerely, then glanced over at Marseahna. "It's time we left."

They made their way stealthily across the wide market square and were just about to disappear into one of the narrow side streets of the old quarter when Marseahna suddenly caught hold of Orion's sleeve, jerking it frantically.

Orion followed Marseahna's gaze reluctantly. There, standing almost in front of them, was a member of the *Star Dancer*'s crew and a squad of Juntarium guards.

They continued walking, almost without hesitation, and had just about reached their escape route when the crew member called out. He raised his arm and pointed at the fleeing figures.

"There they go! Stop them!"

The crowded square cleared of people instantly, except for the two fleeing figures and their pursuers.

Just then a burst from one of the Juntarium trooper's laser weapons glanced off the side of the building near Orion's shoulder. He ducked, but there was a long, narrow unprotected distance ahead of them, and the troopers were almost at their heels.

Another burst of light hit the ground just in front of Marseahna. Deciding now was the time to turn and fight, Orion quickly halted and suddenly spun around, just in time to deflect the energy beam directed at his back. It shot back at an angle just over the troopers' heads.

"We were warned you could deflect a laser beam," one of the Juntarium troopers called out in challenge. "But how about a force of combined laser beams?"

Marseahna stood in Orion's shadow, trembling as she peered over her friend's shoulder. Her brown eyes were as round as the Burganberries she once grew in what might have been another lifetime now.

Marseahna felt Orion take a step backward when the

144

combined force of the Juntarium weapons was trained on him. But still he was able to send the laser rays back at the troopers, who rushed to find shelter from this unique power.

But the *Star Dancer*'s informant didn't have the trained responses of a soldier. When he suddenly realized his own danger, he started to seek shelter in a large metal garbage can, but before he could even get near it, he was struck down and killed at once by a deflected laser beam.

"Careful, captain," one of the troopers warned his vengeful colleague. "We've strict orders not to harm this Auranian prince."

"Don't worry; his natural Aura field will keep him safe from death. But he'll be knocked senseless any minute now," the captain of the troopers predicted. Then a broad smile split his face as he saw what he'd been wating for.

Suddenly Orion jerked forward, looking stunned, and crumbled to the ground. As Marseahna turned around to flee, she was hit by another energy blast from a trooper at the back end of the corridor.

The troopers warily approached the two fallen figures. One of the troopers, with the toe of his boot, turned Orion face upward. The hardened Juntarium troopers were momentarily surprised by the innocent youthfulness of the pale face revealed to them.

"What happens to them now?" the soldier asked, feeling a twinge of pity for these two young people no older than his own son.

The captain shrugged. "Who can say, except that I wouldn't like to be in their place. All I know is that I've orders to take them to the command center," he added in a firm voice. Then he glanced over at the dead body of the Mercai crewman. He signaled to two of his men. "Take care of that body; the rest of you help me with these two."

The trooper who had expressed concern for Orion and Marseahna bent over and started to lift Orion's shoulders when his fingers came into contact with the coldness of metal. He reached underneath the boy and pulled out a chain and the medallion. He looked at the unconscious and oddly touching faces of the young boy and girl, and instead of pocketing the trinket, decided that the young people might need whatever good luck this charm might have. He glanced between the two and placed the pendant over the dark-haired girl's neck, assuming it was hers.

CHAPTER 25

Truestar glanced around the long audience hall in which he'd been standing for over an hour. His eyes were growing weary from the harsh overhead light shining down on his face. He noted the colorful banners decorating one side of the hall, their original emblems now partially hidden by the familiar Juntarium symbol of the scarlet planet, a graphic reminder that these worlds were now part of the Juntarium empire. On the opposite side of the hall were the flags of the newly conquered worlds, their faces also mutilated by the stamp of L'Juntara. It grieved Truestar to see the despoiled flags of Doros, Eraculon, and Govanos, and so many other former Confederation planets.

Truestar sighed, then felt a slight pat on his arm. He glanced over at the woman who'd been standing with him all of this time. How brave Stellara was, he thought sadly. Their time together should have been longer and more meaningful. Neither of them could possibly guess what now awaited them. The gravity of their situation made the days stretch on hopelessly. Since L'Juntara had captured the Exoterra Stone and learned its secrets, he had no need to torture them. Thus far they had been spared the agonizing mental tortures that had made his scientists notorious. How the war was progressing they knew only too well, for L'Juntara had other more subtle methods of breaking a man. Constant bulletins were broadcast to them, keeping them up to date on the latest inevitable Confederate defeat, for there was no defense against the power of the Exoterra Stone.

Truestar was brought out of his thoughts by the sound of marching feet, as the specially uniformed troops of L'Juntara's select guard entered the room and assumed positions along the walls. Their figures were standing at attention and stretched the whole length of the immense hall. A strident blaring of trumpets announced L'Juntara's arrival, and with a flourish only he could command, L'Juntara entered the room, his cloak floating out behind him as he stepped onto the raised platform at the end of the hall. Truestar had to admire the presence of this tall figure with his crown of silver hair, and steel-gray eyes that seemed to hold every eye in the room.

Truestar felt Stellara's fingers grasp his and he tightened his grip comfortingly around her hand as he squarely met L'Juntara's steady gaze. Until this moment the two men had never come face to face, for L'Juntara had personally been commanding his conquering fleet, as they attacked over a dozen worlds. He had not returned to Juntar until now, with complete victory only a battle or two away. The confident dictator now sat down in a large, ornately carved chair that commanded a view of the entire room. The harsh lights overhead cast sharp shadows on his face.

"At last we meet, Truestar," L'Juntara intoned, his voice rich and hypnotic in a manner intended to deceive and disarm his protagonist. "But I doubt whether it is under the conditions you would have preferred. Still, you will allow me my brief moment of triumph, won't you? It was a game well played, though the outcome was never in doubt. For I am destined to rule the galaxy, Truestar, never doubt that. Your days, and those of the Confederation, are finished. But"—L'Juntara smiled, his expression deceptively kind and paternal—"I didn't bring you and the lovely Stellara here to listen to my plans for your worlds—what is left of them, that is— but for a reunion. It was the least I could do for you. You see, I am not completely heartless, my friends."

He nodded at the aide who stood just behind his chair, then folded his arms across his chest, a slight smile of satisfaction curving his cruel lips.

The door he had entered opened once again and a small detail of guards entered. They stepped aside, and

148

Truestar and Stellara could see clearly the figure being escorted by the troopers, his hands bound by an energy neutralizer that flared rays of pain at its victim when any attempt to escape was made. At the sight of the helpless prisoner, Truestar sucked in his breath and took a hesitant step forward. But he was stopped by a guard standing to the left of him. Stellara gasped, feeling relief, then concern, when she recognized the blond head of Orion and his thin, serious face.

The guard was called to a halt a few feet short of where Truestar and Stellara stood. The guard captain stepped forward and gave the hobbled Orion a vicious push, causing him to lose his balance and fall at Truestar's feet. Stellara bent over and helped the prince to his feet, hugging him closely to her side as the three of them stood and faced L'Juntara.

"There is your 'mystic prince,' and now that we have him hostage, I suspect that Aurania will give up without a fight. At least they might be able to save the heir to their throne. He has become somewhat of a legend among my troops for his duel with six of my best soldiers. Unarmed and alone he stood up to them and traded them shot for shot," L'Juntara told them with an unpleasant speculative look at Orion. Now he would wreak his final vengeance on Aurania, that world which had dared to scoff at him, its government refusing to recognize him and his claim to the worlds he had conquered.

Truestar remained silent under L'Juntara's taunting, his hand resting lightly yet firmly on Stellara's shoulder as he tried to restrain her angry reactions. His arm then stretched to protectively enclose the still weakened Orion.

"Where is my friend Marseahna?" Orion's clear voice startled them all, as he stared defiantly into the eyes of L'Juntara, surprised as well by this sudden outburst from the young prince.

"Your show of concern for this Verdanan primitive is admirable but quite puzzling," L'Juntara said. "But in case your concern is genuine," he continued, baiting the young prince, "she happens to be on our first moon, Lucar, where she will spend the rest of her life mining energy crystals for our domed city."

"No!" Orion protested, and stumbled forward, the energy clamps striking out at his flesh with waves of pain. "She's innocent. She's done nothing to harm you."

"Silence! How dare you question me? Your friend was found guilty of aiding and abetting a known Confederate fugitive, a rebel charged with trying to overthrow my power," L'Juntara replied, fuming. "She's hardly innocent, my young prince. Her fate is sealed, but yours," he continued with a sickening smile, "has yet to be decided. Will you plead for your lives? Or will you continue to stand there so bravely and foolishly, hoping for a last-minute reprieve? The Confederacy is dead. There will be no escape for you now."

Truestar pulled Orion back into line with Stellara and himself and shook his gray head sadly. "You are fools. There are still many untold secrets in that turquoise stone upon which you have based your final victories. I would not be so confident just yet, Your Excellency," Truestar chided L'Juntara with an amused smile in his eyes.

L'Juntara narrowed his penetrating gaze on Truestar for a second, then transferred that discomforting stare to his chief aide, who stood nearby. "What is this, general? Is there something I have not been told concerning the Stone of Exoterra?"

The general gritted his teeth as he forced a smile to his tight lips. "Of course not, L'Juntara. The prisoner is just trying to cast doubts. It's his last desperate effort to cause confusion. I'm sure he knows nothing, but I'd be happy to apply the mind probe to this insolent one and discover his true motives," he offered.

"You underestimate my power as well, general," Orion sullenly called, his face flushed with anger and his eyes blazing emerald. "Despite these neutralizing shields, your life is in jeopardy."

Suddenly the general clutched at his throat as the room around him began to shake.

An expression of fear appeared in L'Juntara's eyes. "Stop him at once, Truestar, or I'll have him killed," the dictator commanded, his voice desperate.

Truestar whispered something to the prince and the general's trembling stopped. He regained his breath in a moment, but fear continued to dwell in the eyes of the troopers. They had witnessed a power that even their leader feared.

The tense silence was broken when an aide came hurrying into the room. He rushed right up to the leader, whispering something in L'Juntara's ear. Then he hurried from the room and his leader whispered orders to his general.

"We've just received word from one of our survey craft near the galactic barrier." L'Juntara spoke with a triumphant gleam in his eyes as he stared at the Confederates. "They are registering a very unusual disturbance at the barrier. They think it must be the result of another Exoterra meteor trying to enter our galaxy from the void."

L'Juntara was on his feet in an instant, his face glowing with images of what this would mean to his empire. His eyes met Truestar's, both men reading each other's thoughts in that second. "Take these prisoners at once to our second moon, Secar, where they will be interned for the present time. I will deal with them upon my return. And, my young prince, be assured that I will tear apart your brain until I find the source of the strange power you possess. General, prepare my flagship for immediate flight to the barrier. I want to personally oversee the capture of this new Exoterra Stone."

The Confederates watched as L'Juntara left the hall amid a squadron of his personal guard. All too soon they were in preparation for transport to a shuttle craft for their departure to Secar, the scientific colony that had been established on the second moon of Juntar, a planetoid of frozen wastelands and no native living creatures.

CHAPTER 26

Marseahna lay alone in the small confines of her penal colony cell on the mining moon of Lucar. She was still stunned from the laser beam, and also from the speed with which things had happened. The last thing she remembered was standing behind Orion as he had bravely fought the Juntarium troopers. Then in the next instant she had found herself standing with several other disheveled prisoners who were being sentenced for life to this mining colony on Lucar.

She'd been ordered to the prison barracks, which housed thousands of prisoners from other conquered worlds, and assigned a small, impersonally furnished room. With its barest of essentials, the room seemed like a horrible, nightmarish place to spend the rest of her life. She thought sadly of the lush green fields of Burganberries and the rolling mountains of her farm near Theos. How long ago that seemed now. Feeling a warm trickle of salty tears running down her face, Marseahna hid her head in her arms, wondering what had happened to Orion.

Later she rolled over and stared at the pale shaft of light streaming through the small window in the thick wall. She crawled from the narrow, hard cot and wearily walked over to the window and peered out. From the small opening she could see the lightening sky, a mere ruddy glow that filtered through the haze. In the distance the malevolent atmosphere of Juntar filled the horizon with a rusty hue. Somewhere on that world was Orion, maybe even Stellara and Truestar, if they were all still alive. A humming noise distracted her from her thoughts as she spun around in time to see the security lock slide open to admit a tired-looking man, carrying a tray of provisions.

The man wasn't aware of Marseahna at first, as his eyes adjusted to the darkness of the cell. But when he glanced up, the man suddenly laughed ironically. "A girl! Just a young girl. What did you do, lass, to get yourself thrown in here? Pick flowers from his lordship's palace gardens?"

Marseahna wasn't quite sure of the strange man's meaning, but she felt he must be insulting her in some way. "A person's age or size doesn't determine her politics," Marseahna answered with stilted pride. "I can believe in and die for the Confederate cause just as much as a man of many more years."

The man sat down on the edge of the cot and propped his head up with his hands, a chagrined look on his lean features. "I'm sorry. I had no right to mock you. It's just that you took me by surprise, and I guess I hated seeing one so young confined in this hell hole," he apologized easily. "My name's Drusus; what name do you go by?"

Marseahna curled up in the corner of her cot, still not sure she trusted this Drusus character. "My name is Marseahna," she said coldly, her voice not inviting further conversation, and with a shrug Drusus got up and began to take the provisions off the tray.

Drusus watched the young girl spoon the nutrient-fortified mush into her mouth, her hunger overcoming her initial reluctance to swallow the unappetizing mess.

"Oh, to be young again and able to eat so indiscriminately," Drusus remarked, remembering how he had earlier nearly gagged on a bite of the same food.

Marseahna grinned for the first time. "I'd much prefer to be eating some of my home-baked Burganberry pie—" Marseahna started to say when the chain around her neck broke and the medallion fell into the thick, sticky mass on her plate. It was the first time that Marseahna had become aware of it hanging from her neck, and with a look of surprise she carefully picked it up and began to wipe it off, wondering how she came to

154

have Orion's Delphini medallion. She held it up to the dim light illuminating the cell.

Suddenly Drusus grasped her wrist in a viselike grip. Startled, Marseahna glanced up into the burning eyes of Drusus, his expression causing Marseahna to feel afraid.

"Where did you get that medallion?" Drusus snarled as he pulled Marseahna to her feet and twisted her arm wrenchingly behind her back.

"It's none of your business!" Marseahna cried out, now fiercely protective of the precious medallion that had been mysteriously entrusted to her. Defiantly she stared into Drusus's bleak face.

"I'll break your neck if you don't tell me the truth, daughter of L'Juntara," Drusus threatened meanly.

Marseahna smothered a moan of pain as Drusus continued to twist her arm. "I won't tell you," Marseahna spit out with new-found determination.

"Oh, yes, you will, lass," Drusus insisted as he increased the excruciating pressure of his hold on Marseahna's arm.

Marseahna stared up into those merciless eyes boring into hers. She felt a blackness forming behind her eyes, but was still able to notice something dangling from her attacker's neck. Suddenly she stopped struggling.

Drusus eased his grip slightly, continuing to stare into Marseahna's dark eyes suspiciously, not sure if her capitulation was a trick.

"Alex?" Marseahna squeaked, her voice hoarse with pain and surprise.

Drusus's hands dropped from the limp girl, then reached out and grabbed her as she started to fall. He eased Marseahna down on the edge of her cot and sat down beside her. Then he took her chin in gentle fingers and turned her face to his.

"Say that again," he ordered in words barely above a whisper.

"Are y-you Alex, uncle to Orion?" Marseahna asked with trepidation.

The man sighed deeply at the question. "Who are you?" he then demanded abruptly.

Marseahna slowly described the ordeal that she and her new friends had endured since their fateful meeting in the swamps of Verdana. Alex's eyes widened, their expression intense as he listened closely to the young Verdanan. "The last thing I remember was being in that alley on Juntar. I never saw Orion after that," Marseahna said, gently touching the painful bruises on her arm.

Alex stared at this amazing young girl from Verdana and, shaking his head, he grinned in growing admiration for her. "Orion did make it to Verdana. His Aura shield worked," Alex repeated, his dark blue eyes brimming with tears of joy. "And Truestar knows how to destroy the Exoterra Stone," he added thoughtfully, as if already formulating some plan of action.

"But you're supposed to be dead!" Marseahna insisted. "I only knew it was you because of the Delphini medallion around your neck. I still don't know how I got Orion's pendant."

"Yes, I suppose everyone thinks that I am dead," Alex replied. "I would be, too, if they hadn't salvaged the part of the ship I was in, before it completely broke up. I realized what was happening and changed clothes with one of my crew members, thinking I had a better chance to live if they thought me an ensign of low rank rather than a member of the Auranian royal family. But then I was knocked unconscious, and remember nothing of the journey here. By the time I recovered, I was incarcerated here. Since they thought I was no one of importance, they didn't spare me another glance. I was lucky, or I might have found myself on the other moon, Secar. Very few ever leave there. And after the prisoners are questioned by the mind probes, they come to wish that they were dead."

Alex tapped his fingers ruminatingly on the table. "I have a plan," he offered. "I've noticed that when a shuttle arrives with new prisoners, the security becomes very lax for a few hours. The guards take a break and have a change of duty. A good time for an escape attempt," Alex suggested, a glint of hope burning in his eyes. "You pretend that you are sick and I'll summon a guard. Then we'll jump him, get his weapon, and make for the shuttle craft."

"I'm willing to try, but I don't understand. Why haven't you tried before?" Marseahna asked curiously.

Alex shrugged. "No place to go—and no hope, no purpose. But now we must reach our friends before they are taken to Secar. Secar is the outpost moon, where all prestigious prisoners are taken. There their minds are probed by L'Juntara's cruel instruments. He will stop at nothing in order to understand Orion's Aural power—and his probing will destroy Orion's mind."

"I'm with you," Marseahna said bravely. "Anything is better than spending the rest of my life in this prison. I hope we can somehow help Orion and the others."

The guard who answered the sick call in cell twenty-six, level four, never knew what hit him when he stepped inside the cubicle. Alex quickly disarmed him, stripped him of his uniform, and traded clothes with him.

Alex, posing as the guard, followed Marseahna along the narrow corridors unchallenged, the laser pointed at her back. Marseahna glanced over her shoulder once at the tall figure marching just a foot behind her, then quickly looked straight ahead again. The deadly gleam in Prince Tau-Alexander's eyes was as determined as that of any Juntarium trooper. Marseahna's hope grew as she saw the first step of their plan succeed without a hitch.

Just as they rounded a corner, they suddenly came abreast of two Juntarium troopers standing at ease, gossiping. Marseahna nearly stumbled, crying out in startled protest at the hard shove Alex gave her.

Marseahna cast an indignant look over her shoulder at Alex, her dark eyes eloquent with feeling at having been manhandled.

"Sorry, Marseahna, but I needed to distract their attention from me," Alex replied with a grin that reminded her of Orion.

They quickly found the lift and headed for the top deck and the hangar. Safely inside the elevator, the laser was aimed and ready when the doors opened once again to reveal a large, cavernous chamber where a shuttle craft was docked. Before the curious guards had fully turned around at the sound of their entrance, Alex had fired at them, stunning them before they could even reach for their own weapons.

As Alex had predicted, hangar security was lax. Only a skeleton crew had been on duty guarding the hangar. Alex had often noticed this weak link in security the times he had brought meals up to the guards on duty.

They hurried to the shuttle and were about to board it when Marseahna suddenly cried out in alarm. "My medallion, Alex. It's gone! I had it on the lift but I must have dropped it when I—I'm going back for it. We need the sound tape that Truestar put in it," Marseahna said, running back toward the lift.

"Marseahna, wait!" Alex commanded, but he was too late. She was already running across the hangar, toward the lift.

"Here it is!" she said, picking up the medallion off the floor. As she turned to go back to the shuttle, one of the stunned guards came to and aimed his lethal laser weapon at her back.

"Marseahna, take cover!" Alex yelled, his voice echoing throughout the hangar. "Behind you!"

Alex fired his weapon at the guard, but not before the trooper had unleashed a deadly bolt of energized light at the back of the defenseless girl.

Marseahna fell in her tracks at the base of the shuttle, the medallion still clutched in her fist. Alex reached her and, lifting her up, raced toward the shuttle's open portal. The portal closed securely behind them as Alex laid Marseahna down gently on the cabin floor.

"I was hoping you weren't counting on *me* piloting this shuttle," Marseahna remarked with a painful grin, despite her severe pain.

Alex grinned, reminding Marseahna once again of Orion. "No, I'll take over now," he said, hiding his concern for her injuries. "You just get some well-deserved rest," he added as he activated the control panel, flicking on a series of switches that sent a progression of different-colored lights blinking. "Ready? It's now or never. This is our big chance to become heroes. They'll be writing legends about us after today," Alex joked, trying to take Marseahna's mind off her intense pain.

"The Stone. Orion, I—" she gasped, fading into unconsciousness. Only her barely audible breathing told Alex that she was still alive.

Seconds later Alex piloted the shuttle out of the hangar, lifting higher and higher into the thin atmosphere of Lucar, the rugged surface below becoming an indistinct blur as the small shuttle craft shot into space.

CHAPTER 22

...keep a tremor note in his voice when he had surrendered for...his apartment. He had never lived in...that comforted all those of

CHAPTER 27

Lieutenant Altos glanced down at the visiscreen, which showed Juntar growing smaller in the distance as the shuttle craft he was piloting left orbit and began its short journey to Secar. It had taken considerable restraint to keep a casual note in his voice when he had volunteered for the shuttle assignment. He had never really believed in the deities that comforted so many of his friends. But someone or something had guided this strange meeting in space with the Confederate prisoners, putting him in an ideal position to finally break his cover, and rescue them. He had glanced coldly at the prisoners being marched on board, allowing only a brief flicker of recognition to pass between himself and Stellara, his old Confederate commander. He felt himself perspiring heavily as he went through the long checklist that was standard for lift-off. But finally they had cleared Juntar's hazy red glow, and were now traveling in the cool blackness of space.

"Receiving transmission from Lucar, sir," Altos's co-pilot informed him.

"Lucar?" Altos repeated, fearing that the communication was from L'Juntara.

"They say two prisoners are missing and have commandeered a shuttle craft; they ask us to be on the alert. They are considered dangerous. If possible, we are to intercept them, should they cross our path."

Altos sighed. 'Tell them we are on L'Juntara's personal orders, and transporting prisoners of high security risk. We hardly have the time to chase after reluctant miners."

"Yes, sir!" the young ensign replied, impressed by his pilot's display of authority. He turned and gave the

161

ordered reply. Altos then knocked him out, and the copilot slumped across his communications console.

Leaving the shuttle on automatic, Altos left the cramped bridge and headed back toward the cell containing his prisoners, a smile of anticipation on his face.

"All is not lost," Stellara said as a door slid shut on them and locked them inside the small cabin that served as a cell.

Truestar looked over at her and shook his head. "I do admire your optimism, my dear, but I'm not sure it hasn't been misplaced this time."

"There's something I have to tell you," Stellara said with a wry smile. "The pilot of this shuttle happens to be none other than Altos-Al'Cronus, of Aurania, one of my most trusted officers currently serving as an undercover agent in L'Juntara's starfleet. He nodded at me when we boarded, and I'm sure he will make some effort to take over the ship. With only a four-man crew, his chances are good," she predicted.

"I apologize then. Your optimism was not misplaced." Truestar smiled, giving Stellara a gentle hug. "If Altos can take over the ship, then we are one step closer to our goal, and—"

"Orion, what's wrong?" Stellara cried as she and Truestar rushed to the prince, who had fallen onto the cabin floor, his face distorted with pain. Stellara put Orion's head on her lap and wiped his sweat-laden brow.

"It's Marseahna," Orion said weakly. "She's been injured severely. These energy neutralizers are blocking my perception but I can still feel her pain. And I feel something else. I feel a presence I haven't felt in a long time, but I can't make it out." Orion sighed, growing a bit stronger now that the vision had passed.

"I wish we could get those things off him," Truestar said with anger, glancing at the clamplike machines still around the prince's wrists.

"I'll have them off at once," a voice said as the portal

162

opened, revealing Altos standing over the bodies of the two guards he had just stunned.

"Altos!" Stellara cried out, hugging the Confederate spy. "I knew you wouldn't fail us. It's been such a long time, my friend."

"Commander," he greeted her respectfully, blushing somewhat at the hug she had given him, "it gives me more pleasure than I can tell you to see you safe and well. I'll sure be glad to get out of this Juntarium uniform." His eyes came to rest on Truestar's tall figure and the pale-haired lad standing next to him. "Sir, a pleasure and an honor. Prince Orion, I'll have those machines off you in a second," Altos said, taking a key from his uniform pocket and unfastening the neutralizers. Then he added in a change of tone, "I suggest we make our escape right now. I'd prefer we make our break to deep space before we get any closer to Secar," he advised them.

"Of course; it's time we made our move," Truestar agreed. "We will leave the piloting of this Juntarium shuttle in your hands," he suggested, glancing to Stellara. At her nod of agreement, they followed their rescuer down the corridor and onto the bridge. Soon the copilot and two guards had been secured in the rear cabin and the Confederates began to make plans for their next destination.

Altos changed the course for deep space and waited as Truestar studied the computer star charts. Their destination was limited somewhat, since the shuttle was not equipped with hyperdrive.

"I wish we had a fragment of Exoterra Stone," Truestar said almost wistfully. "It certainly would simplify matters if we could tie into the Juntarium computer network with this shuttle computer and start the chain reaction of self-destruction we've talked about. Our only alternative is to find some planetoid to hide on until we can figure out a way to get hold of a piece of the Stone."

"But we do have some," Altos replied in surprise. "There is a sample of it on board. It's being shipped to Secar for further experimentation," he explained, glanc-

163

ing over at the blond prince. "It was to be used to boost L'Juntara's mind probes and thereby understand the prince's Aura."

"Indeed, you came at the right time, Altos," Truestar said joyfully as he quickly explained the combination of sound, light, and Aura needed to destroy the Exoterra Stone. "Now, if we can tie into the network of Juntarium computers, we can set our plan in motion."

"I can help you with that," Altos said eagerly, happy to be back with his allies. "I know the special computer code that will instantly lock all Juntarium computers together; even the highest-priority messages will be overridden."

"But what about Marseahna, Truestar?" Orion's voice cut through the cabin. "She's been injured. We can't just go off and leave her."

"Orion," Truestar answered sympathetically, his eyes full of understanding, "I know how you must feel, but there is nothing we can do now except put our plan into action. The lives of millions of people depends on what we do *now,* on whether or not we succeed, and that must be our top priority. I'm sorry, Orion, truly I am, and I grieve with you for Marseahna. But if we do succeed in destroying the Exoterra Stone, and L'Juntara with it, then the war will end eventually and we'll be able to seek her release. But now, I'm afraid, is not the time."

Orion nodded his head, wiping at a tear in the corner of his eye. Truestar sighed, wishing there were some way he could help Marseahna.

"The computer is cleared and ready for the special code," Altos announced, returning to his pilot's seat.

"And I've found these flares for the light," Stellara reported, placing them on the bridge console. "Orion, please ready your Aura and give me the recording dot so I can place it in the computer recorder," she requested.

"When we bombard the crystal with the sound, light, and Aura, it will self-destruct, emitting a self-destruct signal that will then be relayed by the computer net-

164

work to every fragment of Exoterra," Truestar verified happily.

Orion reached automatically for the medallion hanging from his neck, and when his fingers didn't encounter it, he felt along his neck for the chain. A horrible realization began to dawn on him as he touched his bare skin.

Truestar saw the look of shock on Orion's face and immediately guessed what was wrong.

"Truestar, I . . ." Orion stuttered. "I don't understand. It was here when Marseahna and I arrived on Juntar. I know I had it when I fought the soldiers in the alley. I had grasped it just before I was knocked unconscious," Orion tried to explain. He felt as if he'd just sentenced them all to death when he stared at their bleak faces.

"Well, it changes quite a few things, but don't blame yourself, Orion," Truestar said, his gray eyes sad. "I guess we'd better find a planet to set down on while I try to figure out those sound tones. It will take some time but I think I can do it," he added optimistically, noting the prince's crestfallen expression.

"One of the troopers probably stole it," Altos said, preparing to change course for a destination they had chosen earlier. "Despite their training, they are still human and—" he was saying when he was interrupted by a message coming in from Secar, questioning their course change. Altos was about to respond when he saw a moving blip on his scanner.

"Investigating stolen shuttle craft from Lucar. Will report findings. Lieutenant Altos signing out," he said in an official abrupt manner. Then, turning to his companions on the bridge, he added, "Some miners have stolen a shuttle craft from Lucar. I think that is what has just shown up on our scanner. At least that gives us a good reason to explain our course change."

Suddenly a bolt of energy rocked their shuttle craft, knocking Truestar and Orion off balance with its shock.

"They're firing on us," Altos relayed with alarm. "It's ironic, because we are more or less on the same

165

side. Of course, they don't know that," he added as he maneuvered the small shuttle out of range of the other craft.

"They must be crazed," Stellara said as she monitored their progress, "or desperate. Why don't you contact them? Warn them off. Tell them we have no intention of trying to stop them."

Altos nodded, opening a channel between the two closing shuttle crafts. "Attention shuttle craft from Lucar. We mean you no harm. We are escaping from Juntar. We are Confederates and wish no fight with you. Please acknowledge. If you do not cease this aggression, we will have to return fire."

They waited in tense silence for several seconds, when suddenly a harsh voice responded across the diminishing space between the two craft. "How do we know this is not a Juntarium trick? That you have not contacted Juntar and informed them of our position? Lower your shields as a sign of good faith," the voice commanded.

Orion felt faint, hearing that familiar voice. It couldn't be. And yet he *was not* dreaming or experiencing a vision. That *was* Alex's voice; he'd swear it was. In fact, that was the presence he'd felt earlier but hadn't been able to see clearly enough to comprehend.

Altos had opened the channel again and was about to reply when Orion leaped forward and cried out, "Alex! Alex! Is it really you?" he yelled, his body shaking with emotion.

Stellara exchanged worried glances with Truestar, who started to put a comforting but restraining arm around the obviously overwrought young prince. "Now, now, Orion, you know it can't be Ale—"

"Orion?" a startled voice came over the communicator. "What kind of trickery is this? Who is that speaking? I demand to know."

Stellara gasped, for she too had recognized the voice at last. "By the moons of Monitarus, I believe Orion is right," she whispered.

166

Altos looked between them in confusion. Could they be talking about Prince Tau-Alexander?

"It's a trick!" Altos warned. "I personally saw Prince Tau-Alexander's ship destroyed over Verdana. The only survivor was an ensign," he said, words clearly carrying to the other shuttle through the open channel.

"It is not a trick, Altos," Alex replied. "And I'm not alone. I have a badly wounded young girl with me who is wearing the Delphini medallion that Truestar gave Orion. She's badly injured. Please believe me and take us aboard quickly. My scanner shows a fleet of Juntarium warships heading this way."

CHAPTER 28

It was a hasty reunion aboard the shuttle as old companions greeted each other warmly. Alex held Orion close, something he had thought he would never get to do again. Marseahna had been carefully transferred aboard as well. The three Juntarium troopers were put back on the ship Alex had been piloting, and it was set adrift in space, with its engines disabled.

Truestar set their plan of action in motion as the fleet of warships closed rapidly on the small craft. Carefully he took the medallion from Marseahna's neck and, pulling the recording dot from behind the Delphini's eye, he put it in the computer link. Then he took the small crystal of Exoterra and placed it in another outlet of the computer.

"Stellara, you take over controls," Truestar ordered. "I need Altos here with me to adjust the computer to transmit the Exoterra self-destruct signal at the same time he activates the high-priority code that will link all computers in the Juntarium network."

Orion stood beside the computer outlet, ready to aim his Aura shield at the crystal. In the corner of the cabin, Alex tended Marseahna, much better now that Orion's Aura field had stopped her internal bleeding. Truestar had noted that none of her vital organs had been damaged and although severely weakened, Marseahna's condition was stable.

"Fleet approaching fast, maneuvering," Stellara called out as she guided the small shuttle through space, preparing for what might seem a very unequal battle. "Message coming across from flagship. Shall I open channels?"

"Yes, we need just a minute to set our effort into motion," Truestar said, standing back and preparing to give the signal for the flares, the recording dot, and Orion's Aura.

The melodious sounds of the Delphini began to fill the cabin just as the Juntarium commander's voice was broadcast to them.

"Confederates! I ask you to surrender at once or, acting in the name of L'Juntara, you will be destroyed here in space. I will personally fire the fir—"

"Now!" Truestar cried, setting into motion a devastating chain of events.

Flares burst into blinding light as all in the cabin shielded their eyes from the intense brightness. The sounds of the Delphini continued to float around the cabin, while Orion trained his eyes and thoughts on the glowing turquoise crystal, whose color looked a sickly green in the glare of the burning flares. Suddenly the stone began to crumble, cracking into harmless bits of fading rock dust, and at that very moment Altos activated the high-priority code that locked all computers in the Juntarium network, including all ships and ground installations. Sensors showed that the crystal of Exoterra that had been destroyed had emitted a strange signal, above the pitch of human hearing. Yet this signal had been transmitted through the linked computers of L'Juntara's dominion.

Something catastrophic was occurring on board all of the warships that had been chasing the shuttle. Several had already fallen behind, their speed decreasing so abruptly that internal explosions were registered by the shuttle scanners. But it was the flagship, which had been the closest, that was suffering the worst effects of the sudden power loss. It was now spinning out of control as several explosions within it were registered on the shuttle scanners. Suddenly the ship just seemed to blow apart as the rebels watched in breathless silence.

Altos switched off the computer and stared around him in disbelief. "We really did it. I don't think I truly believed we could destroy the Exoterra Stone, but we did it. We're free!" he cried out exultantly.

170

"I wonder how L'Juntara is taking this sudden change of fortune," Truestar jokingly asked his companions.

"Not too well, I suspect." Altos smiled, happy at the Confederate success. "Even out at the galactic barrier, his computer is linked to the rest of the network."

"Then he will feel the effects of the loss of Exoterra power as well," Truestar said, wishing he could witness the dictator's furious realization that he'd failed.

"Nearing the galactic barrier, my Supreme Commander," the captain informed L'Juntara, who was in the copilot's seat of his flagship. "The disturbance is still strong. Registering it off to our port side."

"Move in closer; with the Exoterra Stone powering us, we can slide right through the energy field of the barrier. Prepare tractor beams to pick up any Exoterra meteors," L'Juntara ordered with a glowing light in his eyes as he anticipated his next glorious victory.

"The first meteors are appearing," the captain said with excitement, anticipating a command of his own someday, with warships all powered by the strange turquoise stone. "Registering on our scanners as Ex—no" —the captain corrected himself—"as a combination of ores, and common to *our* galaxy. It's just a meteor shower that has somehow gotten off course in the barrier. It is not the Exoterra Stone, my Supreme Commander," he informed L'Juntara, wishing he did not have to be the bearer of such disappointing news.

L'Juntara bolted from his seat. Now he loomed over the visiscreen threatening to crush it beneath his fist as he gazed at what was just an ordinary meteor shower.

"No," he murmured, refusing to accept this demoralizing turn of events. "There have to be more turquoise stones. I must have a whole empire fueled with Exoterra power," he insisted, unable to acknowledge this setback to his imperial conquest of the galaxy. He continued to peer intently at the chunks composed of plain metallic ores, his eyes straining to catch even the slightest flash of turquoise.

"L'Juntara"—the captain broke into his thoughts—"something has altered our computer into the special high-priority code position. There is a strange signal coming thr—"

Suddenly the ship was rocked by a violent explosion, sending L'Juntara off balance and against the visiscreen.

"What's happening?" he yelled as his pilot fought to maintain their course and the ship lurched out of control, carrying them into the heart of the barrier. L'Juntara braced himself against the bulkhead, his face mirroring disbelief and horror, while his flagship spun around and around in its fast-approaching rendezvous with the unknown force within the barrier.

"We've lost our Exoterra power," the pilot called out, fear now uppermost in his mind as he saw strange gaseous shapes swirl past them. L'Juntara's finest flagship now shot into the unexplored depths of the galactic barrier, and as the pilot glanced over his shoulder, abandoning his attempts to control the ship, his eyes widened at the look of extreme terror gripping his Supreme Commander's face, now that of a madman. A pinkish-green glow was staining the bridge with a nightmarish quality —then there was only darkness engulfing them.

CHAPTER 29

Orion let the warm sand slip through his fingers, pretending he had all the time in the galaxy to just lie there on the beach and let his mind drift. How suddenly conditions had changed. Truestar and Alex had gotten into immediate contact with Aurania, informing them of the destruction of the Exoterra Stone and requesting transport to rescue them. Their short-range shuttle had run out of fuel when the Confederates had fled into deep space to avoid the fall-out from the destruction of L'Juntara's fleet. The whereabouts of L'Juntara himself remained a mystery. Extensive scouting of the barrier region by Confederation vessels had revealed no sign of the dictator. He was presumed lost in the wilds of the barrier, crushed by that massive field's magnetic strengths.

Without a leader, the Juntarium league began to crumble. Confederation forces were already reconquering territories lost to L'Juntara. On Juntar, itself, a revolution had occurred. The domed cities elected a democratic council to govern them. Doros and the other damaged Confederation planets were already in the process of rebuilding, and healing the wounds that the war had caused.

With only a brief stop on Ceanius, to drop off certain personnel, the Auranian ship had traveled on to Aurania, where key Confederate leaders gathered to wipe out the last remnants of Juntarium opposition. Under the wise guidance of Truestar, Stellara, and Prince Tau-Alexander, all seemingly risen from the dead in the Confederates' most desperate hour, they would now accept nothing less than total victory. Aided by Altos's valuable information about the inner workings and troop movements of L'Juntara's empire, the Confederates' job was made considerably easier.

Orion glanced out beyond the breakwaters, where the Delphini and the dark head of the now recovered Marseahna could be seen bobbing up and down, swimming among the wind-swept waves from the warm offshore flow. He recalled the joyous reunion with the Delphini.

"Thank you; we were, of course, pleased to see you again. Not that we really had any doubts," Xenos said confidently, reading Orion's thoughts.

"Well, I wish I'd been as certain," Orion replied aloud. "I'm sorry that we must be leaving so soon. Marseahna feels that she must go home to help her people in their sudden transition to the modern world. She stands to become a wealthy dealer in Burganberries, now that Verdana has been opened as a port for free trade. And soon it will become a Confederation member."

"She is correct. She will be needed on her home world. But you will meet again, young prince. She does love you very much," Xenos said, edging up against the prince in the shallows. *"And you and the Delphini will always be good friends; never fear about that."*

"That's the one thing I never had any fear about." Orion laughed, hugging the Delphini close to him. "And what is in store for me, Xenos? Can you predict that?"

"At first I see you back in the columned palace on Aurania, bringing strength and leadership to your people once again. But it won't be long before you set off on another adventure, for I had a vision of you many star systems away. That is all I know."

"Just enough to tease me with, eh, Xenos? All right, take me out beyond the breakwater. After all this teasing, the least you can do is give me a free ride."

Orion stared up at the turquoise sky, the color soft and luminous and not at all threatening. Xenos glided the prince out to where Marseahna and many other Delphini frolicked in the sea swells.

"Come on, Marseahna," Orion taunted. "Xenos and I'll beat you to the shallows."

"We'll see about that. Come on, Rielos, let's go!" Marseahna laughed as they began to race back to shore.

And in the last rays of day, the sky faded to dark turquoise. The first evening star appeared to witness the winner of the race.

GORDON McBAIN was born in California and has lived in Germany, Alabama, Louisiana, and Georgia. Mr. McBain now makes his home in Los Angeles, California, where he works as a high school counselor. Mr. McBain has always been an avid fan of space adventures, and THE PATH OF EXOTERRA is his first novel.